U0084476

序 言

　　本書自第一冊出版以來，深受各界好評，聽力測驗的訓練，愈多愈好。學生只有在參加模擬測驗的時候，才會專心，上聽力課，才不會睡覺。

　　英語能力分級檢定測驗依不同英語程度，分為初、中、中高、高和優等五級，預計施測時間為兩個小時，一般民眾通過中級英語能力檢定測驗之後，可以此做為就業或申請學校的證明。教育部待這項測驗發展穩定後，結合大學入學考試，擴充認證制度功能。

　　第二冊書分為八回，每回考試時間為 40 分鐘，每回測驗分為四部份，和教育部的中級英語檢定測驗相同。本書適合高中畢業程度使用。

　　本書是依據「英語能力分級檢定」測驗指標，在單字為五千字的範圍內，可聽懂對話及廣播。要在聽力一項得高分，就是要不斷練習，現在在校的高中學生，要及早準備，為學校爭光。本書另附有教學專用本。

編者 謹識

本書製作過程

　　Test　Book　No. 9, 12, 15 由謝靜芳老師負責，Test Book No. 10, 13, 16 由蔡琇瑩老師負責，No. 11, 14 由高瑋謙老師負責。每份試題均由三位老師，在聽力班實際測驗過，經過每週一次測驗後，立刻講解的方式，學生們的聽力有明顯的進步，在大學甄試聽力考試中，都輕鬆過關。三位老師們的共同看法是，要在聽力方面得高分，就要不斷練習，愈多愈好。聽力訓練，愈早開始愈好。

　　本書另附有教學專用本，售價 120 元。
　　錄音帶八卷，售價 960 元。

English Listening Comprehension Test

Test Book No. 9

This listening comprehension test will test your ability to understand spoken English. In this test, each conversation, statement and question will be spoken JUST ONE TIME. They will not be written out for you. There are four parts to this test. Special instructions will be given to you at the beginning of each part.

Part A

In Part A, you will see several pictures in your test book. For each picture, you will be asked 1 to 3 questions. For each question, you will hear four possible answers. Choose the best answer according to what you see in the picture.

Example:

<u>You will see:</u>

<u>You will hear:</u>   What is this?
                      A. This is a table.
                      B. This is a chair.
                      C. This is a watch.
                      D. This is a doll.

The best answer to the question "What is this?" is B: "This is a chair." Therefore, you should choose answer B.

A. Questions 1-3

D. Questions 8-9

B. Question 4

E. Questions 10-12

C. Questions 5-7

F. Questions 13-15

Part B

In Part B, you will hear 15 questions. After you hear a question, read the four possible answers in your test book and decide which one is the best answer to the question you have heard.

Example:

<u>You will hear:</u> What does your father do?

<u>You will read:</u> A. He's 50 years old.
  B. He's a teacher.
  C. He's hungry.
  D. He's in Los Angeles.

The best answer to the question "What does your father do?" is B: "He's a teacher." Therefore, you should choose answer B.

Please go to the next page. ⇨

16. A. I am so surprised.
    B. Of course, you got it.
    C. Yes, I mean it.
    D. You have to study hard.

17. A. My friends are.
    B. They are singing.
    C. There is one boy in the classroom.
    D. They are my classmates.

18. A. It's too little to spend.
    B. A deal is a deal.
    C. Will that be cash?
    D. Thank you very much.

19. A. May I help you?
    B. Can I do you a favor?
    C. What size of Coke, sir?
    D. What would you like?

20. A. By car.
    B. Once a week.
    C. Two times.
    D. Eight hours a day.

21. A. Cheer up!
    B. That's all right.
    C. Thank you.
    D. You are very kind.

22. A. They had a good time.
    B. For an hour.
    C. About two weeks.
    D. At three o'clock.

23. A. What did you lose?
    B. We'll lose a lot of money.
    C. Don't worry. We can ask the boy over there.
    D. I don't know how much we lost.

24. A. Yes, it's their house.
    B. Yes, they are.
    C. No, they are our house.
    D. No, it's their house.

25. A. My chair is broken.
    B. My watch was lost.
    C. I have good luck.
    D. Yes, no problem.

26. A. Yes, there are any birds
      in it.
    B. No, there are not some.
    C. Yes, there are some.
    D. Yes, there is some.

27. A. Am I?
    B. You did?
    C. Thank you.
    D. Oh, my goodness.

28. A. How do you know it?
    B. Of course, they are not
      enough.
    C. Sure, more than enough.
    D. Who are you talking
      about?

29. A. That's all right.
    B. I'll come here again.
    C. I got up late.
    D. I am so surprised.

30. A. Sometimes I go by bus,
      and sometimes by bicycle.
    B. The bus is faster; bicycles
      are too slow.
    C. I never ride my bicycle
      to work.
    D. I sometimes work on
      Sunday.

Part C

In Part C, you will hear 15 conversations between a man and a woman. After each conversation, you will hear a question about the conversation. After you hear the question, read the four possible answers in your test book and choose the best answer to the question you have heard.

Example:

You will hear: (Man)   How do you go to school every day?

           (Woman)   Usually by bus. Sometimes by taxi.

           TONE: How does the woman go to school?

You will read: A. She always goes to school on foot.
               B. She usually takes a bike.
               C. She takes either a bus or a taxi.
               D. She usually goes to school by bus, never by taxi.

The best answer to the question "How does the woman go to school?" is C: "She takes either a bus or a taxi." Therefore, you should choose answer C.

Please go to the next page. ⇨

31. A. Finish checking his
       references.
    B. Complete the research.
    C. Put the material in order.
    D. Finish typing the paper.

32. A. Go to the lab briefly.
    B. Check on what's for dinner.
    C. Go running before they eat.
    D. See if they have plenty
       of work.

33. A. Write.
    B. Study.
    C. Shop.
    D. Eat.

34. A. He doesn't keep his promises.
    B. He's very trustworthy.
    C. He's not really busy.
    D. Phil will help.

35. A. The tickets were gone.
    B. The play was bad.
    C. The sale wasn't interesting.
    D. The weather was too cold.

36. A. In a library.
    B. In a bookstore.
    C. In a post office.
    D. In a supermarket.

37. A. He fell.
    B. He had a fight.
    C. He was killed.
    D. He was punished.

38. A. Writing checks for tickets.
    B. A train trip.
    C. Today's rainstorm.
    D. Using their tickets.

39. A. If he'll have time to eat
       in Chicago.
    B. Where the bus station is
       located.
    C. When buses depart for
       Chicago.
    D. If he can catch a bus that
       leaves Chicago.

40. A. A garage.
    B. A doctor's office.
    C. A dentist's office.
    D. A construction company.

41. A. In a spacecraft.
    B. On the moon.
    C. In an observatory.
    D. In an astronomy class.

42. A. It might rain.
    B. She's afraid of open windows on trains.
    C. Her suitcase is too full to close.
    D. The drains are clogged up.

43. A. Pick things up.
    B. Wash the floor.
    C. Write a book.
    D. Lie down.

44. A. It's filled with lies.
    B. It doesn't describe all her experience.
    C. It is too long.
    D. It contains one lie.

45. A. He should run more.
    B. He asks too many questions.
    C. He wants to be president.
    D. He has a good imagination.

Part D

In Part D, you will hear 15 short talks. After each talk, you will hear a question about the talk. After you hear the question, read the four possible answers in your test book and choose the best answer to the question you have heard.

Example:

You will hear: Well, that's all for Unit 15. For today's
                  homework, please do the review questions on
                  page 80, and we'll check the answers tomorrow.
                  Now, let's go on to Unit 16.

                  TONE: What is the teacher going to do next in
                      today's class?

You will read: A. Check the homework.
                  B. Review Unit 15.
                  C. Start a new unit.
                  D. Answer students' questions.

The best answer to the question "What is the teacher going to do next in today's class?" is C: "Start a new unit." Therefore, you should choose answer C.

Please go to the next page. ⇨

46. A. The giant bird cage.
    B. The tiger house.
    C. The monkey and ape
       habitat.
    D. The tropical rainforest
       exhibit.

47. A. From affluent merchants.
    B. From his father.
    C. From classes at school.
    D. From his co-workers.

48. A. A dance club.
    B. A student arts committee.
    C. A group of professors.
    D. A sports team.

49. A. It would be too long.
    B. It would be more difficult
       to read.
    C. It could not be copied
       easily.
    D. It could not be handed in
       on time.

50. A. A telephone.
    B. A person.
    C. A communication system.
    D. A television.

51. A. Cutting a field.
    B. Talking with newsmen.
    C. Jogging.
    D. Fishing.

52. A. 98.6.
    B. 37.
    C. Body temperature.
    D. A temperature scale.

53. A. A frying pan.
    B. An omelet.
    C. A telephone.
    D. A fair.

54. A. At a store.
    B. At a warehouse.
    C. In a video arcade.
    D. In a school.

55. A. 10 points.
    B. 2 points.
    C. 15 points.
    D. 5 points.

56. A. Radios.
    B. Coins for telephones.
    C. Palmtop computers.
    D. Ordinary beepers.

57. A. A doctor.
    B. A circus act.
    C. A bilingual aide.
    D. A clown.

58. A. The home team won.
    B. It ended in a tie.
    C. The crowd ruined the game.
    D. The Rams won.

59. A. A concert pianist.
    B. A builder.
    C. A jazz musician.
    D. An astronaut.

60. A. At a concert.
    B. At a sports event.
    C. At a bank.
    D. At a stage play.

Listening Test 9 詳解

Part A

For questions number 1 to 3, please look at picture A.

1. (**C**) Question number 1, where is the burning building?
    A. It is next to the stadium.
    B. It is on the freeway.
    C. It is on the traffic circle.
    D. It is out of town.
    * stadium ('stedɪəm) *n.* 體育館　　*traffic circle* 圓環

2. (**B**) Question number 2, please look at picture A again. How busy is the stadium?
    A. The stadium is full.
    B. The stadium is nearly empty.
    C. The stadium is crowded.
    D. The stadium is packed.
    * packed (pækt) *adj.* 擠滿人的

3. (**C**) Question number 3, please look at picture A again. What is in the sky?
    A. There is a balloon in the sky.
    B. There is a flying saucer in the sky.
    C. There is a helicopter in the sky.
    D. There is a flock of birds in the sky.
    * balloon (bə'lun) *n.* 氣球　　*flying saucer* 飛碟
    helicopter ('hɛlɪ,kɑptɚ) *n.* 直升機　　flock (flɑk) *n.* （鳥）群

For question number 4, please look at picture B.

4. (**C**) Question number 4, what time is it?
    A. It is one o'clock.　　 B. It is five past two.
    C. It is five past twelve.　　D. It is five to twelve.

For questions number 5 to 7, please look at picture C.

5. (**D**) Question number 5, where are they?
   A. They are at the beach.
   B. They are at a snack bar.
   C. They are on a farm.
   D. They are in a park.

   * *snack bar* 小吃店

6. (**C**) Question number 6, please look at picture C again.　How is the weather?
   A. It is cold and windy.
   B. It is warm and rainy.
   C. It is warm and windy.
   D. It is cold and sunny.

   * windy ('wɪndɪ) *adj.* 有風的

7. (**B**) Question number 7, please look at picture C again.　What is the man doing?
   A. He is selling ice cream.
   B. He is taking a picture.
   C. He is taking a walk.
   D. He is talking with the women.

   * *take a picture* 照像　*take a walk* 散步

For questions number 8 to 9, please look at picture D.

8. (**B**) Question number 8, where are they?
   A. They are in a park.
   B. They are on a campus.
   C. They are in an airport.
   D. They are in a zoo.

   * campus ('kæmpəs) *n.* 校園

9. (**B**) Question number 9, please look at picture D again. How is the graduate?

    A. He is pessimistic.

    B. He is happy.

    C. He is crying.

    D. He is angry.

    * graduate ('grædʒuɪt) *n.* 大學畢業生
      pessimistic (,pɛsə'mɪstɪk) *adj.* 悲觀的

For questions number 10 to 12, please look at picture E.

10. (**B**) Question number 10, what is this a picture of?

    A. It is a picture of a hotel lobby.

    B. It is a picture of a snack bar.

    C. It is a picture of an airport.

    D. It is a picture of a bank.

    * lobby ('labɪ) *n.* 大廳

11. (**A**) Question number 11, please look at picture E again. What do the two women have in common?

    A. They both have a ponytail.

    B. They both have ice cream.

    C. They both have a bag.

    D. They both have a drink.

    * ponytail ('ponɪ,tel) *n.* 馬尾

12. (**C**) Question number 12, please look at picture E again. What food can't you buy here?

    A. Soda.

    B. Popcorn.

    C. Fried rice.

    D. Coffee.

    * soda ('sodə) *n.* 汽水   *fried rice* 炒飯

For questions number 13 to 15, please look at picture F.

13. (**C**) Question number 13, what is next to BALTON'S?
    A. It is the post office.
    B. It is a bakery.
    C. It is a flower shop.
    D. It is a police station.
    * bakery ('bekərɪ) *n.* 麵包店

14. (**D**) Question number 14, please look at picture F again. What is behind the bakery?
    A. It is a florist.
    B. It is a school.
    C. It is a temple.
    D. It is a church.
    * florist ('florɪst) *n.* 花店

15. (**B**) Question number 15, please look at picture F again. What is in front of the post office?
    A. There is a school.
    B. There are four mailboxes.
    C. There are two police cars.
    D. There is a park.
    * mailbox ('mel,bɑks) *n.* 郵筒；信箱

Part B

16. (**A**) Believe it or not, I got the best grades in the English test.
    A. I am so surprised.
    B. Of course, you got it.
    C. Yes, I mean it.
    D. You have to study hard.
    * *You got it.* 你懂了。   *I mean it.* 我是認眞的。

17. (**A**) Who is studying English?
　　　A. My friends are.
　　　B. They are singing.
　　　C. There is one boy in the classroom.
　　　D. They are my classmates.

18. (**C**) I'd like to pay for this.
　　　A. It's too little to spend.
　　　B. A deal is a deal.
　　　C. Will that be cash?
　　　D. Thank you very much.
　　　A deal is a deal. 一言為定。　　cash (kæʃ) *n.* 現金

19. (**C**) I'd like a small order of French fries and a Coke.
　　　A. May I help you?
　　　B. Can I do you a favor?
　　　C. What size of Coke, sir?
　　　D. What would you like?
　　　French fries 薯條

20. (**B**) How often do you go to the movies?
　　　A. By car.
　　　B. Once a week.
　　　C. Two times.
　　　D. Eight hours a day.

21. (**B**) I'm sorry that I can't lend you the money.
　　　A. Cheer up!
　　　B. That's all right.
　　　C. Thank you.
　　　D. You are very kind.
　　　Cheer up! 振作精神！

22. (**D**) What time did the students go home?
> A. They had a good time.
> B. For an hour.
> C. About two weeks.
> D. At three o'clock.

23. (**C**) Oh, I am sorry. I am afraid we are lost.
> A. What did you lose?
> B. We'll lose a lot of money.
> C. Don't worry. We can ask the boy over there.
> D. I don't know how much we lost.

24. (**A**) May, is that Mr. and Mrs. Wang's house?
> A. Yes, it's their house.
> B. Yes, they are.
> C. No, they are our house.
> D. No, it's their house.

25. (**A**) What's the matter with you?
> A. My chair is broken.
> B. My watch was lost.
> C. I have good luck.
> D. Yes, no problem.
>
> * broken ('brokən) *adj.* 壞了的

26. (**C**) Are there any birds in the tree?
> A. Yes, there are any birds in it.
> B. No, there are not some.
> C. Yes, there are some.
> D. Yes, there is some.

27. (C) You speak very good English.

    A. Am I?

    B. You did?

    C. Thank you.

    D. Oh, my goodness.

    * *My goodness*! 天啊！(= *My God!*)

28. (C) Do you have enough money to buy the sweater?

    A. How do you know it?

    B. Of course, they are not enough.

    C. Sure, more than enough.

    D. Who are you talking about?

29. (A) I'm sorry I am late.

    A. That's all right.

    B. I'll come here again.

    C. I got up late.

    D. I am so surprised.

30. (A) How do you go to work?

    A. Sometimes I go by bus, and sometimes by bicycle.

    B. The bus is faster; bicycles are too slow.

    C. I never ride my bicycle to work.

    D. I sometimes work on Sunday.

Part C

31. (C) W: How are you coming on your research paper?

    M: I've finished all my research, but I haven't been able to organize it. I have to do that before I can write the paper.

(TONE)

Q: What does the man have to do now?

A. Finish checking his references.

B. Complete the research.

C. Put the material in order.

D. Finish typing the paper.

* **come on** 進展　　**research paper** 研究報告
  reference〔'rɛfərəns〕*n.* 參考資料　　**put ~ in order** 整理好~

32. (**A**) W: Can you drop by the lab for a minute? I have some
experiments running that I need to check on before dinner.
M: Sure, I have plenty of time. I'd be interested to see what
you are working on anyway.

(TONE)

Q: What will they do?

A. Go to the lab briefly.

B. Check on what's for dinner.

C. Go running before they eat.

D. See if they have plenty of work.

* **drop by** 順道拜訪　　lab〔læb〕*n.* 實驗室 (= *laboratory*)
  experiment〔ɪk'spɛrəmənt〕*n.* 實驗　　**work on** 進行；從事
  briefly〔'briflɪ〕*adv.* 短暫地　　**see if ~** 看看究竟~

33. (**D**) W: Let's go out for pizza or hamburgers or something. I'm
tired of writing.
M: Good, I need to take a break from studying, too.

(TONE)

Q: What are they planning to do now?

A. Write.　　　　　B. Study.

C. Shop.　　　　　D. Eat.

* **or something** 或什麼的　　**take a break** 休息一下

34. (**A**) M: Phil said he would help me if he has time.

W: He often offers his help, but he never seems to have time.

(TONE)

Q: What does the woman say about Phil?

A. He doesn't keep his promises.

B. He's very trustworthy.

C. He's not really busy.

D. Phil will help.

* *keep one's promise* 遵守諾言

trustworthy〔'trʌst,wɜðɪ〕*adj.* 值得信賴的

35. (**A**) M: We were going to go to the theater Saturday. But unfortunately the play we were most interested in is all sold out.

W: That's too bad. Why don't you try to get tickets for another night?

(TONE)

Q: Why was the man disappointed?

A. The tickets were sold out.

B. The play was called off.

C. The play wasn't interesting.

D. The weather was too cold.

* play〔ple〕*n.* 戲劇 *sold out* 賣完的 *call off* 取消

36. (**C**) W: This package must be insured and sent to the United States. Would you weigh it for me?

M: Certainly. That will be two dollars and seventy cents all together.

(TONE)

Q: Where does this conversation probably take place?

A. In a library. B. In a bookstore.

C. In a post office. D. In a supermarket.

* insure〔ɪn'ʃur〕*v.* 保險 weigh〔we〕*v.* 稱重

37. (**A**) M: Your son is only badly bruised. In a couple of days he'll
            be well enough to go back to climbing trees.
        W: He won't be climbing any more trees if I can help it.
            A fall like that could have killed him.

    (TONE)
    Q: What happened to the boy?
    A. He fell.
    B. He had a fight.
    C. He was killed.
    D. He was punished.
    　* badly ('bædlɪ) *adv.* 嚴重地　　bruise (bruz) *v.* 瘀血
    　　fight (faɪt) *n.* 打架

38. (**D**) W: This ticket is a rain check. What does that mean?
        M: If it had rained today and the game had been postponed,
            you could have used your ticket on a new date.

    (TONE)
    Q: What is the couple discussing?
    A. Writing checks for tickets.
    B. A train trip.
    C. Today's rainstorm.
    D. Using their tickets.
    　* *rain check* 雨天換票證；改天再招待
    　　postpone (post'pon) *v.* 延期　　couple ('kʌpl̩) *n.* 兩人；夫婦
    　　rainstorm ('ren,storm) *n.* 暴風雨

39. (**C**) M: Do you know if the bus station has a timetable for buses
            to Chicago?
        W: They may not, but I know you can catch a bus that leaves
            for Chicago every day at 10:00 A.M.

(TONE)

Q: What does the man want to find out?

A. If he'll have time to eat in Chicago.

B. Where the bus station is located.

C. When buses depart for Chicago.

D. If he can catch a bus that leaves Chicago.

* timetable ('taɪm,tebḷ) n. 時間表　**find out** 查出
  locate (lo'ket) v. 位於　**depart for** 開往

40. (**C**) M: During my examination I found that you have two cavities
which need to be filled.　Also, your wisdom teeth ought
to be taken out.

W: Oh no!　I was hoping I would not have to see you again
until my next annual checkup.

(TONE)

Q: Where did this conversation take place?

A. A garage.　　　　　　B. An airport.

C. A dentist's office.　　D. A construction company.

* cavity ('kævətɪ) n. 洞　**wisdom tooth** 智齒
  annual ('ænjuəl) adj. 一年一度的　checkup ('tʃɛk,ʌp) n. 健康檢查
  dentist ('dɛntɪst) n. 牙醫　**construction company** 建設公司

41. (**A**) M: The moon is really beautiful from here.

W: Especially when it's the first time you have seen it from so
far above the Earth.

(TONE)

Q: Where did this conversation probably take place?

A. In a spacecraft.　　　B. On the moon.

C. In an observatory.　　D. In an astronomy class.

* spacecraft ('spes,kræft) n. 太空船
  observatory (əb'zɜvə,torɪ) n. 天文台
  astronomy (əs'trɑnəmɪ) n. 天文學

42. (**A**) M: Let's get going, dear. What is taking so long?
W: I'm closing the window in case it rains.

(TONE)
Q: What does the woman mean?
A. It might rain.
B. She's afraid of open windows on trains.
C. Her suitcase is too full to close.
D. The drains are clogged up.
> * suitcase (ˈsutˌkes) *n.* 手提箱　　drain (dren) *n.* 排水管
> clog (klɑg) *v.* 阻塞

43. (**A**) W: Ted, why are all these books and clothes lying all over
the floor?
M: I'm sorry. I'll clean up right now.

(TONE)
Q: What will Ted do?
A. Pick things up.　　　　B. Wash the floor.
C. Write a book.　　　　D. Lie down.
> * lie (laɪ) *v.* 在　　***clean up*** 打掃乾淨；整理

44. (**B**) M: According to your résumé, you don't have much experience
in advertising, Miss Smith.
W: That's not quite true. My father was an advertising
consultant and he gave me a fairly thorough introduction
to the business.

(TONE)
Q: What does Miss Smith say about her résumé?
A. It's filled with lies.
B. It doesn't describe all her experience.
C. It is too long.
D. It contains one lie.
> * résumé (ˌrɛzʊˈme) *n.* 履歷表　　consultant (kənˈsʌltənt) *n.* 顧問
> fairly (ˈfɛrlɪ) *adv.* 非常地　　thorough (ˈθɝo) *adj.* 徹底的

45. (**C**) M: Do you think Bill will run for the presidency?
　　　　　W: I imagine it's just a question of time before he makes his announcement.

(TONE)
Q: What does the woman think about Bill?
A. He should run more.
B. He asks too many questions.
C. He wants to be president.
D. He has a good imagination.

　* **run for** 競選　　presidency (ˈprɛzədənsɪ) n. 總統職位

Part D

46. (**A**) The show will be at 4:30 in the giant bird cage, where Dr. Smith will give a guided tour, pointing out more than 300 species of birds from Central and South America.

(TONE)
Q: What will Dr. Smith give a guided tour of?
A. The giant bird cage.
B. The tiger house.
C. The monkey and ape habitat.
D. The tropical rainforest exhibit.

　* giant (dʒaɪnt) adj. 巨大的　　guided (ˈgaɪdɪd) adj. 有導遊的
　　species (ˈspiʃɪz) n. 種　　habitat (ˈhæbə‚tæt) n. 棲息地
　　tropical rainforest 熱帶雨林　　exhibit (ɪgˈzɪbɪt) n. 展覽

47. (**B**) Today we're going to discuss the architect Samuel Brown, a man from New York, who lived during the latter half of the eighteenth century. Mr. Brown had very little formal training; he learned his skill from his father, a carpenter, and from architectural books.

(TONE)

Q: How did Samuel Brown learn his skill?

A. From affluent merchants.

B. From his father.

C. From classes at school.

D. From his co-workers.

* architect (ˈɑrkəˌtɛkt) n. 建築師　　carpenter (ˈkɑrpəntɚ) n. 木匠
  affluent (ˈæfluənt) adj. 富裕的　　merchant (ˈmɝtʃənt) n. 商人
  co-worker (ˈkoˈwɝkɚ) n. 同事

48. (**A**) Attention everyone. The university dance club is going to begin offering weekend classes in stilt walking. If you've never tried walking on stilts, this is your chance. You will suddenly be transformed into a nine-foot tall giant, and you'll feel like you are walking among the trees and the clouds.

(TONE)

Q: What organization is offering the event?

A. A dance club.

B. A student arts committee.

C. A group of professors.

D. A sports team.

* club (klʌb) n. 社團　　stilt (stɪlt) n. 高蹺
  transform (trænsˈfɔrm) v. 轉變　　giant (dʒaɪnt) n. 巨人
  event (ɪˈvɛnt) n. 大型活動　　sports (spɔrts) adj. 運動的
  committee (kəˈmɪtɪ) n. 委員會

49. (**B**) Your paper should be at least five pages long and it must be typed. I don't want any handwritten papers because sometimes they are too hard to read. I hope all of you've begun writing your papers already.

(TONE)

Q: Why should the paper not be handwritten?

A. It would be too long.
B. It would be more difficult to read.
C. It could not be copied easily.
D. It could not be handed in on time.

* handwritten (ˈhændˌrɪtn̩) adj. 手寫的   copy (ˈkɑpɪ) v. 模仿
   hand in 繳交   *on time* 準時

50. (**C**) The air is filled with thousands of voices using MAX's 3300 number to call around the world every day. MAX can put you in touch with people within seconds, no matter where you are.

(TONE)

Q: What is MAX?

A. A telephone.
B. A person.
C. A communication system.
D. A television.

* communication (kəˌmjunəˈkeʃən) n. 通訊

51. (**C**) Brian Jameson reports that while the President was home in Plains over the weekend, he went out jogging in the morning, as is customary for him to do.

(TONE)

Q: What was the President doing on that weekend morning?

A. Cutting a field.
B. Talking with newsmen.
C. Jogging.
D. Fishing.

* customary (ˈkʌstəmˌɛrɪ) adj. 習慣性的
   cut (kʌt) v. 穿越   newsman (ˈnjuzmən) n. 新聞記者

52. (**D**) Fahrenheit is used in the United States whereas many European countries use centigrade. This can be very confusing for people who are obviously used to centigrade. The normal body temperature in centigrade is 37 whereas in Fahrenheit it is 98.6.

(TONE)

Q: What is Fahrenheit?

A. 98.6.

B. 37.

C. Body temperature.

D. A temperature scale.

  * Fahrenheit (ˈfærənˌhaɪt) *n.* 華氏溫度計
    whereas (hwɛrˈæz) *conj.* 然而   centigrade (ˈsɛntəˌgred) *adj.* 攝氏的
    scale (skel) *n.* 刻度；衡量標準

53. (**B**) Welcome to Cooking Fair. Today, we're going to demonstrate how to make an omelet, using your teflon-coated frying pan.

(TONE)

Q: What will the cook make?

A. A frying pan.

B. An omelet.

C. A telephone.

D. A fair.

  * fair (fɛr) *n.* 博覽會   demonstrate (ˈdɛmənˌstret) *v.* 示範
    omelet (ˈɑmlɪt) *n.* 煎蛋捲   teflon (ˈtɛfˌlɑn) *n.* 鐵氟龍
    coat (kot) *v.* 塗在…上   ***frying pan*** 煎鍋；平底鍋

54. (**B**) Today, we will begin sending out Game Kid video games. Orders have been heavy, so there are more games to send in each shipment than usual. All orders must go out today.

(TONE)

Q: Where is this announcement being made?

A. At a store.   B. At a warehouse.
C. In a video arcade.   D. In a school.

* *video games* 電動玩具   heavy (ˈhɛvɪ) *adj.* 大量的
shipment (ˈʃɪpmənt) *n.* 出貨   announcement (əˈnaʊnsmənt) *n.* 宣布
warehouse (ˈwɛrˌhaʊs) *n.* 倉庫
arcade (arˈked) *n.* 商店街；遊樂中心

55. (**D**) I ask that each of your papers be typed. Besides, I count off
points for various kinds of mistakes. A misspelled word will
cost you 5 points. You've lost 25 points if you've misspelled
five words.

(TONE)

Q: How many points will a student lose if he misspells a word
on a composition?

A. 10 points.   B. 2 points.
C. 15 points.   D. 5 points.

* misspell (mɪsˈspɛl) *v.* 拼錯
composition (ˌkampəˈzɪʃən) *n.* 作文

56. (**D**) Airox has offered a great variety of pagers. Now, they are
all unnecessary. Our new palmtop computer can receive
pager messages directly. It can send out replies from coin
telephones. You can rid yourself of separate pagers.

(TONE)

Q: What does this product make unnecessary?

A. Radios.   B. Coins for telephones.
C. Palmtop computers. D. Ordinary beepers.

* pager (ˈpedʒɚ) *n.* 呼叫器   palmtop (ˈpamˌtap) *adj.* 掌上型的
coin telephone 公共電話   *rid sb. of sth.* 使某人免除某物
beeper (ˈbipɚ) *n.* 呼叫器

57. (**C**) Does anyone in the audience speak Chinese? We need someone to interpret Chinese and English for medical personnel.
We will bring you to the Grand Circus as scheduled, but one
performer will be unable to perform. If you can help, please
see a theater usher.

(TONE)
Q: What is this request for?
A. A doctor.　　　　　　　B. A circus act.
C. A bilingual aide.　　　　D. A clown.

 * interpret (ɪn'tɜprɪt) v. 翻譯　　personnel (ˌpɜsn̩'ɛl) n. 人員
 circus ('sɜkəs) n. 馬戲團　　schedule ('skɛdʒul) v. 預定
 usher ('ʌʃɚ) n. 引導員；帶位人員　　act (ækt) n. 節目
 bilingual (baɪ'lɪŋgwəl) adj. 能說兩種語言的
 aid (ed) n. 助手　　clown (klaʊn) n. 小丑

58. (**A**) In tonight's hockey game, the visiting Rams came out hot and
scored two goals in the first three minutes. The Mountaineers,
however, came out of their locker room in the second period
and skated like they'd never lost a game to the Rams. The
crowd went wild when the Mountaineers finally beat the Rams,
four to three.

(TONE)
Q: What was the final outcome of the game?
A. The home team won.
B. It ended in a tie.
C. The crowd ruined the game.
D. The Rams won.

 * hockey ('hɑkɪ) n. 曲棍球　　visiting ('vɪzɪtɪŋ) adj. 作客的
 a visiting 客隊 (↔ a home team 地主隊)　　hot (hɑt) v. 猛烈的
 score (skor) v. 得分　　goal (gol) n. 一分
 locker room （更衣用的）櫥櫃間　　period ('pɪrɪəd) n. 局；場
 beat (bit) v. 打敗　　tie (taɪ) n. 平手
 ruin (ruɪn) v. 破壞

59. (**C**) Louis Armstrong was one of the best known and best loved jazz musicians in the United States. He was also known for his "great, happy smile" and his gravelly voice. Wherever he went, his concerts sold out. His hometown, New Orleans, is considered the home of jazz.

(TONE)

Q: Who was Louis Armstrong?

A. A concert pianist.

B. A builder.

C. A jazz musician.

D. An astronaut.

* jazz〔dʒæz〕*n.* 爵士樂　　gravelly〔'ɡrævəlɪ〕*adj.* 低沈沙啞的
home〔hom〕*n.* 發源地　　astronaut〔'æstrə,nɔt〕*n.* 太空人

60. (**D**) The seats marked with red covers are reserved. The doors will be kept closed except between acts. Please turn off pagers and cellular phones. Photography, videotaping and audiotaping are strictly prohibited. This evening's performance will run until 10:15. There will be a brief intermission after Act Two.

(TONE)

Q: Where is this announcement being made?

A. At a concert.

B. At a sports event.

C. At a bank.

D. At a stage play.

* mark〔mɑrk〕*v.* 作記號　　cover〔'kʌvɚ〕*n.* 套子
reserve〔rɪ'zɝv〕*v.* 預訂　　act〔ækt〕*n.* 幕
cellular phone 行動電話　　videotape〔'vɪdɪo,tep〕*v.* 錄影
audiotape〔'ɔdɪo,tep〕*v.* 錄音　　prohibit〔pro'hɪbɪt〕*v.* 禁止
intermission〔,ɪntɚ'mɪʃən〕*n.* 休息時間
sports event 運動競賽　　***stage play*** 舞台劇

English Listening Comprehension Test

Test Book No. 10

This listening comprehension test will test your ability to understand spoken English. In this test, each conversation, statement and question will be spoken JUST ONE TIME. They will not be written out for you. There are four parts to this test. Special instructions will be given to you at the beginning of each part.

Part A

In Part A, you will see several pictures in your test book. For each picture, you will be asked 1 to 3 questions. For each question, you will hear four possible answers. Choose the best answer according to what you see in the picture.

Example:

You will see:

You will hear: What is this?
  A. This is a table.
  B. This is a chair.
  C. This is a watch.
  D. This is a doll.

The best answer to the question "What is this?" is B: "This is a chair." Therefore, you should choose answer B.

A. **Questions 1-3**

B. **Questions 4-6**

C. **Questions 7-9**

D. **Questions 10-12**

E. **Questions 13-15**

Part B

In Part B, you will hear 15 questions. After you hear a question, read the four possible answers in your test book and decide which one is the best answer to the question you have heard.

Example:

<u>You will hear</u>:   What does your father do?

<u>You will read</u>:   A. He's 50 years old.
B. He's a teacher.
C. He's hungry.
D. He's in Los Angeles.

The best answer to the question "What does your father do?" is B: "He's a teacher." Therefore, you should choose answer B.

Please go to the next page. ⇨

16. A. I am afraid I can't.
    B. No, we'd love to.
    C. We're going to.
    D. I am afraid so.

17. A. I am sorry to do so.
    B. No, thanks.
    C. I'd be happy to help.
    D. Yes, thank you.

18. A. They are all six for five
       cents.
    B. Yes, they are cheap.
    C. All right.　I'll buy six.
    D. It costs fifty cents.

19. A. That's a good idea.
    B. Yes, thanks.
    C. Yes, tea is cheaper.
    D. Coffee, please.

20. A. Are you?
    B. Where, where.
    C. Thank you.
    D. You are right.

21. A. Let me to see it.
    B. Really?　Have you got a
       computer?
    C. When did you bought it?
    D. How much you cost it?

22. A. I like vacation very much.
    B. I have no idea.
    C. It always comes in February.
    D. Everything is all right.

23. A. That's all right.
    B. Well, you can go.
    C. Why must we go?
    D. It sounds great.

24. A. Forty years old.
    B. He's fine, thank you.
    C. He's old.
    D. A bus driver.

25. A. At nine-forty.
    B. In the evening.
    C. I usually go to bed at ten.
    D. I sometimes go to bed late.

26. A. My brother does.
    B. My sister will.
    C. My mother did.
    D. My father has.

27. A. No, he isn't.
    B. No, I think not.
    C. No, I don't think it.
    D. No, I think so.

28. A. He gets up every morning.
    B. He usually goes to school at 7:00.
    C. He gets up early.
    D. He usually gets up at 6:30.

29. A. Yes, I do. I do have two sisters.
    B. No, I don't. I have only two brothers.
    C. No, she doesn't. She has two sisters.
    D. Yes, she does. She has two sisters.

30. A. Because we have to study on Monday.
    B. We have a lot of free time on that day.
    C. It will rain on Monday.
    D. Some friends came to visit me on Monday.

Part C

In Part C, you will hear 15 conversations between a man and a woman. After each conversation, you will hear a question about the conversation. After you hear the question, read the four possible answers in your test book and choose the best answer to the question you have heard.

Example:

<u>You will hear:</u>   (Man)   How do you go to school every day?
                (Woman)   Usually by bus. Sometimes by taxi.

                TONE: How does the woman go to school?

<u>You will read:</u>   A. She always goes to school on foot.
                B. She usually takes a bike.
                C. She takes either a bus or a taxi.
                D. She usually goes to school by bus, never by taxi.

The best answer to the question "How does the woman go to school?" is C: "She takes either a bus or a taxi." Therefore, you should choose answer C.

Please go to the next page. ⇨

31. A. To mail a letter and a
       check.
    B. To buy stamps.
    C. To get a package.
    D. To draw a check to the
       postman.

32. A. Use prepared cake mixes.
    B. Cut another piece of cake.
    C. Start baking from scratch.
    D. Buy a moist cake.

33. A. He works three times as
       much as he did before.
    B. He has two free days for
       every three days he works.
    C. He works three nights
       every two weeks.
    D. He has twice as much
       work as he used to have.

34. A. He will get angry.
    B. He is looking for a parking
       space.
    C. He has to buy a parking
       ticket.
    D. He will discover it himself.

35. A. Only if it is always in sight.
    B. No, because she asked
       him to turn it off between
       problems.
    C. He should leave it on the
       table.
    D. No, because he asked
       for it.

36. A. Because you must take
       the stairs.
    B. Because nine is an odd
       number.
    C. Because the elevator got
       stuck.
    D. Because there are too many
       people in the elevator.

37. A. Because it is customary.
    B. Because he had extra
       money.
    C. Because the lady lost her
       money by mistake.
    D. Because the musician took
       a shower.

38. A. The vacation has been
       too long.
    B. The lady smells musty.
    C. The lady smells something
       musty.
    D. The windows are open.

39. A. 7:10
    B. 7:00
    C. 6:50
    D. 7:05

40. A. The brothers have moved
       away.
    B. It is not his affair.
    C. The brothers don't know.
    D. He doesn't know the way.

41. A. In an electrical shop.
    B. At a college.
    C. In an airport.
    D. At a voting booth.

42. A. A field trip.
    B. A hut in the woods.
    C. A bad dream.
    D. A footrace.

43. A. She is pitiful.
    B. She is too shy to apply.
    C. They are afraid of her.
    D. She is intelligent.

44. A. They haven't seen any.
    B. They have seen enough.
    C. They can't afford one.
    D. They have an apartment.

45. A. She feels bad.
    B. She hasn't been to dinner.
    C. Her boyfriend has been
       at her house all day.
    D. Jane is having dinner.

Part D

In Part D, you will hear 15 short talks. After each talk, you will hear a question about the talk. After you hear the question, read the four possible answers in your test book and choose the best answer to the question you have heard.

Example:

<u>You will hear</u>:   Well, that's all for Unit 15. For today's homework, please do the review questions on page 80, and we'll check the answers tomorrow. Now, let's go on to Unit 16.

TONE: What is the teacher going to do next in today's class?

<u>You will read</u>:   A. Check the homework.
B. Review Unit 15.
C. Start a new unit.
D. Answer students' questions.

The best answer to the question "What is the teacher going to do next in today's class?" is C: "Start a new unit."   Therefore, you should choose answer C.

Please go to the next page. ⇨

46. A. She took art lessons.
    B. She went to lots of museums.
    C. She went swimming with her friends.
    D. She took swimming lessons.

47. A. A president.
    B. A filmmaker.
    C. An author.
    D. An actor.

48. A. She doesn't teach mathematics.
    B. She has a good sense of humor.
    C. She likes George very much.
    D. She has many friends.

49. A. In high school.
    B. When he entered college.
    C. After his second year of high school.
    D. After his second year of college.

50. A. She takes care of the layout.
    B. She's the general editor.
    C. She's in charge of the fiction page.
    D. She edits the cooking page.

51. A. A market research company.
    B. A news agency.
    C. A dating agency.
    D. A private detective agency.

52. A. The toy department.
    B. The pet department.
    C. The women's jeans department.
    D. The women's sportswear department.

53. A. Information about immigration.
    B. A visa.
    C. A landing card.
    D. Duty-free goods.

54. A. It's going to cease to exist in some areas.
    B. It's going to improve on the whole.
    C. It's going to be flooded with competition.
    D. It's going to develop in Florida.

55. A. Cathy's family visited Mami.
    B. Cathy came to see Mami
       from Scotland.
    C. Mami enjoyed her holiday
       in Switzerland.
    D. Mami had a good time in
       Scotland.

56. A. Thursday, June 2.
    B. Saturday, June 4.
    C. Thursday, June 23.
    D. Saturday, June 25.

57. A. An optometrist.
    B. A professor.
    C. A pharmacist.
    D. A dentist.

58. A. Tower A and B.
    B. Tower C.
    C. Tower D.
    D. Tower E.

59. A. As a liquid medicine.
    B. As a drink in ceremonies.
    C. As a health drink mixed
       with sugar.
    D. As a popular drink.

60. A. About 6%.
    B. About 16%.
    C. About 60%.
    D. About 66%.

Listening Test 10 詳解

Part A

For questions number 1 to 3, please look at picture A.

1. (**A**) Question number 1, what is next to the falling man?
   A. A fire hydrant.
   B. A stop sign.
   C. A van.
   D. A door.

   * ***fire hydrant*** 消防栓 ***stop sign*** 紅燈
    van (væn) *n.* 有蓋貨車

2. (**C**) Question number 2, please look at picture A again. Why is the man falling down?
   A. He stepped in a puddle.
   B. He tripped on the ice.
   C. He slipped on the ice.
   D. He walked on the puddle.

   * puddle (ˋpʌdḷ) *n.* 水坑
    trip (trɪp) *v.* 絆倒 slip (slɪp) *v.* 滑倒

3. (**B**) Question number 3, please look at picture A again. What is in the background?
   A. There is a sidewalk.
   B. There is a bridge.
   C. There is a fire hydrant.
   D. There are some trees.

   * background (ˋbæk͵graʊnd) *n.* 背景
    sidewalk (ˋsaɪd͵wɔk) *n.* 人行道

For questions number 4 to 6, please look at picture B.

4. (**B**) Question number 4, what are the kids sitting on?

    A. They are sitting on a chair.
    B. They are sitting on a sofa.
    C. They are sitting on a bench.
    D. They are sitting on the floor.

    * bench (bɛntʃ) *n.* 長凳

5. (**C**) Question number 5, please look at picture B again. What is the man wearing glasses holding?

    A. He is holding a cigar.
    B. He is holding a glass.
    C. He is holding a child.
    D. He is holding a toy.

6. (**A**) Question number 6, please look at picture B again. What is the girl giving the boy?

    A. She is giving him a present.
    B. She is giving him a pillow.
    C. She is giving him a flower.
    D. She is giving him a dog.

    * present ('prɛznt) *n.* 禮物

For questions number 7 to 9, please look at picture C.

7. (**B**) Question number 7, where are they?

    A. They are in the living room.
    B. They are in the kitchen.
    C. They are in the hall.
    D. They are in the yard.

8. (**D**) Question number 8, please look at picture C again.　What
is the man giving the woman?
A. He is giving her a sink.
B. He is giving her a stove.
C. He is giving her a screw driver.
D. He is giving her a bill.

screw driver 螺絲起子

9. (**C**) Question number 9, please look at picture C again.　What is
the man?
A. He is a doctor.
B. He is a writer.
C. He is a plumber.
D. He is a mechanic.

* plumber (ˈplʌmɚ) *n.* 水管工人　　mechanic (məˈkænɪk) *n.* 技師

For questions number 10 to 12, please look at picture D.

10. (**B**) Question number 10, where is the woman sitting?
A. She is sitting on the sofa.
B. She is sitting in the armchair.
C. She is sitting on the carpet.
D. She is sitting behind the TV.

* carpet (ˈkɑrpɪt) *n.* 地毯

11. (**D**) Question number 11, please look at picture D again.　What is
the woman doing?
A. She is watching TV.
B. She is playing with a dog.
C. She is sleeping.
D. She is reading a newspaper.

12. (**A**) Question number 12, please look at picture D again.　What is in front of the sofa?
　　A. There is a table.
　　B. There is a TV.
　　C. There is a picture.
　　D. There is a telephone.

For questions number 13 to 15, please look at picture E.

13. (**C**) Question number 13, what is this a picture of?
　　A. It is a restaurant.
　　B. It is a chicken.
　　C. It is a kitchen.
　　D. It is a garage.
　　* garage (gəˋrɑʒ) *n.* 車庫;修車廠

14. (**B**) Question number 14, please look at picture E again.　What is number 1?
　　A. It is a closet.
　　B. It is a cupboard.
　　C. It is a stove.
　　D. It is a drawer.
　　* closet (ˋklɑzɪt) *n.* 衣櫥　　cupboard (ˋkʌbəd) *n.* 碗櫥
　　drawer (drɔr) *n.* 抽屜

15. (**A**) Question number 15, please look at picture E again.　What is number 11?
　　A. It is a stove.
　　B. It is an oven.
　　C. It is a sink.
　　D. It is a refrigerator.
　　* oven (ˋʌvən) *n.* 烤箱

Part B

16. (**A**) I am having a party this Sunday. Can you come?
    A. I am afraid I can't.
    B. No, we'd love to.
    C. We're going to.
    D. I am afraid so.

17. (**C**) Would you like to help me to pack?
    A. I am sorry to do so.
    B. No, thanks.
    C. I'd be happy to help.
    D. Yes, thank you.

    * pack〔pæk〕v. 打包；整理行李

18. (**A**) How much are these cookies?
    A. They are all six for five cents.
    B. Yes, they are cheap.
    C. All right. I'll buy six.
    D. It costs fifty cents.

19. (**D**) Would you like some tea or coffee?
    A. That's a good idea.　　B. Yes, thanks.
    C. Yes, tea is cheaper.　　D. Coffee, please.

20. (**C**) You are so smart.
    A. Are you?　　　　　　B. Where, where.
    C. Thank you.　　　　　D. You are right.

21. (**B**) That's my computer.
    A. Let me to see it.
    B. Really? Have you got a computer?
    C. When did you bought it?
    D. How much you cost it?

22. (**B**) What are your plans for vacation?
  - A. I like vacation very much.
  - B. I have no idea.
  - C. It always comes in February.
  - D. Everything is all right.

23. (**D**) Let's go on a picnic next Sunday.
  - A. That's all right.
  - B. Well, you can go.
  - C. Why must we go?
  - D. It sounds great.

24. (**B**) How is your father?
  - A. Forty years old.
  - B. He's fine, thank you.
  - C. He's old.
  - D. A bus driver.

25. (**A**) What time did you go to bed yesterday?
  - A. At nine-forty.
  - B. In the evening.
  - C. I usually go to bed at ten.
  - D. I sometimes go to bed late.

26. (**B**) Who will help you do your homework?
  - A. My brother does.　　B. My sister will.
  - C. My mother did.　　D. My father has.

27. (**A**) Do you think John is right?
  - A. No, he isn't.
  - B. No, I think not.
  - C. No, I don't think it.
  - D. No, I think so.

28. (**D**) What time does your brother get up?

    A. He gets up every morning.

    B. He usually goes to school at 7:00.

    C. He gets up early.

    D. He usually gets up at 6:30.

29. (**D**) Does Mary have any sisters?

    A. Yes, I do.　I do have two sisters.

    B. No, I don't.　I have only two brothers.

    C. No, she doesn't.　She has two sisters.

    D. Yes, she does.　She has two sisters.

30. (**A**) Why don't you have your birthday party on Monday?

    A. Because we have to study on Monday.

    B. We have a lot of free time on that day.

    C. It will rain on Monday.

    D. Some friends came to visit me on Monday.

Part C

31. (**A**) W: Are you going to the post office for stamps or to pick up a package?

    M: Neither.　I left a letter for the postman to take yesterday, but he left it clipped to the mailbox.　And this check has got to be in the mail today.　I'd better hurry.

    (TONE)

    Q: Why is the man going to the post office?

    A. To mail a letter and a check.

    B. To buy stamps.

    C. To get a package.

    D. To draw a check to the postman.

    * ***pick up*** 領　　package ('pækɪdʒ) *n.* 包裹

    clip (klɪp) *v.* 夾住　　***draw a check*** 開支票

32. (**C**) M: This cake is simply delicious.　I never knew you were
　　　　 such a good cook.
　　　　 W: It is moist, isn't it?　But the credit should go to Betty
　　　　 Crocker and her prepared cake mix.　If it weren't for her,
　　　　 I'd never bake.　Oh, let me cut you some more.

　　　　 (TONE)
　　　　 Q: What is the woman unable to do?
　　　　 A. Use prepared cake mixes.
　　　　 B. Cut another piece of cake.
　　　　 C. Start baking from scratch.
　　　　 D. Buy a moist cake.

　　　　 * moist〔mɔɪst〕*adj.* 濕潤的（指在烤箱中烤的時間剛好）
　　　　　 credit〔'krɛdɪt〕*n.* 信用；功勞
　　　　　 start from scratch 從頭開始

33. (**B**) W: I'm sure glad I don't have your job.　Working all night
　　　　 and sleeping in the daytime.
　　　　 M: Oh, I stopped that when I got my promotion.　Now I'm on
　　　　 three days and off two.

　　　　 (TONE)
　　　　 Q: How does the man work now?
　　　　 A. He works three times as much as he did before.
　　　　 B. He has two free days for every three days he works.
　　　　 C. He works three nights every two weeks.
　　　　 D. He has twice as much work as he used to have.

　　　　 * promotion〔prə'moʃən〕*n.* 升遷

34. (**A**) M: Mr. Smith has a parking ticket on his car.
　　　　 W: Don't tell him about it.　He'll become furious.　Let him
　　　　 discover it himself.

(TONE)

Q: Why doesn't the woman want to tell Mr. Smith about the parking ticket?

A. He will get angry.

B. He is looking for a parking space.

C. He has to buy a parking ticket.

D. He will discover it himself.

* ticket ('tɪkɪt) *n.* 罰單　　furious ('fjʊrɪəs) *adj.* 憤怒的

35. (**B**) M: May I borrow your hand calculator?

W: Yes, but be sure to turn it off between each problem so the battery doesn't wear out.

(TONE)

Q: Should the man leave the calculator on all afternoon?

A. Only if it is always in sight.

B. No, because she asked him to turn it off between problems.

C. He should leave it on the table.

D. No, because he asked for it.

* *wear out* 用完　　*in sight* 在視線內；看得見

36. (**B**) W: Does this elevator stop on every floor?

M: No, it stops only on the even ones.　If you want an odd one, go to the even one above it and then walk down.

(TONE)

Q: Why won't the elevator stop on the ninth floor?

A. Because you must take the stairs.

B. Because nine is an odd number.

C. Because the elevator got stuck.

D. Because there are too many people in the elevator.

* even ('ivən) *adj.* 雙數的；偶數的

odd (ɑd) *adj.* 單數的；奇數的　　stick (stɪk) *v.* 卡住

37. (**A**) W: I thought you threw the money by mistake.

M: Oh, no, you are supposed to shower the musicians with money to show you liked the music.

(TONE)

Q: Why did the man throw money toward the musicians?

A. Because it is customary.

B. Because he had extra money.

C. Because the lady lost her money by mistake.

D. Because the musician took a shower.

* *by mistake* 弄錯　　*be supposed to* 應該
customary (ˈkʌstəˌmɛrɪ) *adj.* 習慣的

38. (**C**) W: Let's not stay long here.　This house smells musty.

M: Naturally.　It has been vacant for a long time.　We'll keep the windows open while we inspect it.

(TONE)

Q: Why does the lady refuse to stay here?

A. The vacation has been too long.

B. The lady smells musty.

C. The lady smells something musty.

D. The windows are open.

* musty (ˈmʌstɪ) *adj.* 發霉的　　vacant (ˈvekənt) *adj.* 空著的
inspect (ɪnˈspɛkt) *v.* 檢查

39. (**C**) M: Is dinner ready?　Grandfather always starts eating at seven on the dot.

W: I just have to add the vegetables and cook everything for five minutes.　Afterwards we'll have five more minutes to serve everything.

(TONE)

Q: What time is it?

A. 7:10　　B. 7:00　　C. 6:50　　D. 7:05

* *on the dot* 準時　　serve (sɜv) *v.* 準備；上菜

40. (**B**)　W: Did the Jones brothers stop talking to each other?
　　　　　　M: It's none of my business, so I can't say one way or the other.

　　　　　　(TONE)
　　　　　　Q: Why doesn't the man answer the question?
　　　　　　A. The brothers have moved away.
　　　　　　B. It is not his affair.
　　　　　　C. The brothers don't know.
　　　　　　D. He doesn't know the way.

41. (**B**)　M: Rita is taking a course in music.
　　　　　　W: I wish I could.　I could fit only one elective into my
　　　　　　　　schedule, so I chose art.

　　　　　　(TONE)
　　　　　　Q: Where did this conversation most likely take place?
　　　　　　A. In an electrical shop.
　　　　　　B. At a college.
　　　　　　C. In an airport.
　　　　　　D. At a voting booth.

　　　* elective (ɪˋlɛktɪv) n. 選修科目　　schedule (ˋskɛdʒul) n. 課表
　　　　 electrical shop 電器行　　***voting booth*** 投票亭

42. (**C**)　W: What happened next?
　　　　　　M: Next I dreamt that my feet turned into wood, and would
　　　　　　　　not run, and so I could not escape.

　　　　　　(TONE)
　　　　　　Q: What is the man describing?
　　　　　　A. A field trip.
　　　　　　B. A hut in the woods.
　　　　　　C. A bad dream.
　　　　　　D. A footrace.

　　　* ***field trip*** 實地調查旅行　　hut (hʌt) n. 小屋
　　　　 footrace (ˋfʊt͵res) n. 競走

43. (**D**) M: She wants to apply for the job, but she is really not qualified,
I'm afraid.

W: That's a pity.　She seems so bright.　Don't you think we
could train her?

(TONE)

Q: Why might the applicant receive on-the-job training?

A. She is pitiful.

B. She is too shy to apply.

C. They are afraid of her.

D. She is intelligent.

* ***on-the-job training*** 在職訓練　　pitiful (ˈpɪtɪfəl) *adj.* 可憐的

44. (**C**) M: Have you found an apartment yet?

W: No.　We need such a large amount of space that all the
apartments we've seen are too expensive.

(TONE)

Q: Why are the people having trouble finding an apartment?

A. They haven't seen any.

B. They have seen enough.

C. They can't afford one.

D. They have an apartment.

45. (**A**) M: I haven't seen Jane all day.

W: I think she's upset because her boyfriend isn't coming to
the dinner tonight.

(TONE)

Q: What is the matter with Jane?

A. She feels bad.

B. She hasn't been to dinner.

C. Her boyfriend has been at her house all day.

D. Jane is having dinner.

Part D

46. (**D**) Emi loves going to art museums. She usually goes to a museum every Sunday, but during her summer holidays she began taking swimming lessons on Sundays. So she went to only two museums all summer.

   (TONE)
   Q: What did Emi do on Sundays during her summer holidays?
   A. She took art lessons.
   B. She went to lots of museums.
   C. She went swimming with her friends.
   D. She took swimming lessons.

47. (**C**) Welcome to Viewpoint. On last week's program we talked with filmmaker Michael Chambers about his new documentary on the 1960s. Now if you didn't get enough of the 1960s on our last program, stay tuned, because in just a moment, we'll be chatting with Maria Keene, author of a new biography on President John F. Kennedy.

   (TONE)
   Q: Who is going to be on the program?
   A. A president.
   B. A filmmaker.
   C. An author.
   D. An actor.

   * documentary (ˌdɑkjə'mɛntərɪ) *n.* 記錄片　***stay tuned*** 不要轉台

48. (**B**) George likes all of the teachers in his high school. But his favorite is Miss Johnson, who teaches mathematics. He likes her because she has a good sense of humor and is very friendly.

(TONE)

Q: Why does George like Miss Johnson so much?

A. She doesn't teach mathematics.

B. She has a good sense of humor.

C. She likes George very much.

D. She has many friends.

49. (**D**) Mark played soccer in high school. When he went to college, he continued to play soccer. Mark loved soccer, but after his second year of college he decided to stop playing. It was taking too much time. He wanted to have more time to study.

(TONE)

Q: When did Mark decide to stop playing soccer?

A. In high school.

B. When he entered college.

C. After his second year of high school.

D. After his second year of college.

50. (**D**) Jack, let me introduce you to the staff members in our section. This is Sarah. She edits the cooking and fashion pages. Jim here takes care of the general design and layout. Clare deals with fiction and readers' letters, and I'm in charge-- which means I do everything no one else wants to do!

(TONE)

Q: What does Sarah do?

A. She takes care of the layout.

B. She's the general editor.

C. She's in charge of the fiction page.

D. She edits the cooking page.

* section ('sɛkʃən) *n.* 部門　　edit ('ɛdɪt) *v.* 編輯
  layout ('le,aʊt) *n.* 版面設計　　*deal with* 處理
  fiction ('fɪkʃən) *n.* 小說　　*be in charge* 負責管理

51. (**D**)　This is Thompson and Clark Investigation Agency.　No one is in the office to take your call at the moment, but you can reach our mobile service 24 hours a day at 7223-3314.　Alternatively, you can leave a message here after the tone and we'll get right back to you.

(TONE)
Q: What kind of company is this?
A. A market research company.
B. A news agency.
C. A dating agency.
D. A private detective agency.

* investigation〔 ɪnˌvɛstə'geʃən 〕*n.* 調查　*investigation agency* 徵信社
mobile〔'mobɪl 〕*adj.* 機動的　*mobile phone* 大哥大
alternatively〔 ɔl'tɜnətɪvlɪ 〕*adv.* 或者
market research 市場調查　*news agency* 通訊社
dating agency 婚友社　*private detective* 私家偵探

52. (**D**)　Good afternoon, and thank you for shopping at J-Mart.　We have a lost little boy in the women's sportswear department who says his name is Jimmy.　He has brown hair and brown eyes, and is wearing a Turtles T-shirt and blue jeans.　Would his mother please report to the information desk immediately?

(TONE)
Q: What department is the lost boy in?
A. The toy department.
B. The pet department.
C. The women's jeans department.
D. The women's sportswear department.

* *information desk* 詢問台

53. (**C**) If you travel by air, you will be given a landing card while in
flight, to present to the immigration officials at your destination.
Do not forget to fill it out completely and have it ready with
your passport when you go through immigration.

(TONE)
Q: What will you receive on the airplane?
A. Information about immigration.
B. A visa.
C. A landing card.
D. Duty-free goods.

* ***landing card*** 入境卡　　present (prɪ'zɛnt) v. 交給
immigration (,ɪmə'greʃən) n. 入境處
official (ə'fɪʃəl) n. 人員　　destination (,dɛstə'neʃən) n. 目的地
fill out 填寫　　***go through*** 通過

54. (**A**) Global warming will ultimately end the real estate business in
lowlying coastal regions.　As temperatures increase and the
icecaps begin to melt, rising sea levels will begin to cause
flooding in what are now some of the prime development
areas, such as Florida and other states in the Gulf area.

(TONE)
Q: What is going to happen to the real estate industry?
A. It's going to cease to exist in some areas.
B. It's going to improve on the whole.
C. It's going to be flooded with competition.
D. It's going to develop in Florida.

* global ('globḷ) *adj.* 全球的
ultimately ('ʌltəmɪtlɪ) *adv.* 最後　　***real estate*** 房地產
lowlying ('lo,laɪɪŋ) *adj.* 低窪的　　coastal ('kostḷ) *adj.* 沿岸的
icecap ('aɪs,kæp) n. 冰蓋　　melt (mɛlt) v. 融化
sea level 海平面　　prime (praɪm) *adj.* 精華的
gulf (gʌlf) n. 海灣　　***the Gulf*** 墨西哥灣
be flooded with 充滿

55. (**D**) Last summer Mami visited her friend Cathy in Scotland. During her stay, Cathy and her family took Mami to the rivers, lakes and mountains nearby. Everything was wonderful and very new to Mami, and she enjoyed the natural beauty of the area. It was an unforgettable summer for her.

(TONE)

Q: What happened to Mami last summer?

A. Cathy's family visited Mami.

B. Cathy came to see Mami from Scotland.

C. Mami enjoyed her holiday in Switzerland.

D. Mami had a good time in Scotland.

56. (**B**) I just wanted to remind everyone that this Saturday, June 4, is our annual company picnic. As you know, this year we're holding it at Oakmont Park. In case you haven't signed up yet, just give Gloria Travis a call at ext. 452 no later than Thursday. Also, if you're planning to car pool, we'll be meeting in front of the main office at 8:30 a.m.

(TONE)

Q: When is the company picnic scheduled for?

A. Thursday, June 2.

B. Saturday, June 4.

C. Thursday, June 23.

D. Saturday, June 25.

* annual ('ænjuəl) *adj.* 年度的

   in case 萬一；如果   *sign up* 簽名加入

   ext. = extension (ɪk'stɛnʃən) *n.* 分機   *car pool* 共乘

57. (**A**) Your eyes are fine, Miss Carter, but your prescription must be updated. Your farsightedness has deteriorated so you'll need stronger lenses and maybe bifocals.

(TONE)

Q: Who is speaking?

A. An optometrist.

B. A professor.

C. A pharmacist.

D. A dentist.

* prescription (prɪ'skrɪpʃən) n. 藥方　　update (ʌp'det) v. 更新
farsightedness ('far'saɪtɪdnɪs) n. 遠視
deteriorate (dɪ'tɪrɪə,ret) v. 惡化　　lens (lɛnz) n. 鏡片
bifocals (baɪ'fok̩z) n.pl. 雙焦點的眼鏡；遠近兩用的眼鏡
optometrist (ɑp'tɑmətrɪst) n. 驗光師；配鏡師
pharmacist ('farməsɪst) n. 藥劑師　　dentist ('dɛntɪst) n. 牙醫

58. (**A**) Thank you for calling the University Residence and Off-Campus Housing office. Our university offers five on-campus residences called Towers A,B,C,D, and E. Freshmen are only accepted in Towers A and B. Other year students and graduate students can apply to any Tower.

(TONE)

Q: Which Towers can freshman students apply for?

A. Tower A and B.

B. Tower C.

C. Tower D.

D. Tower E.

* residence ('rɛzədəns) n. 住宅　　***off-campus*** 校外的
graduate student 研究所學生

59. (**B**) Human beings tasted chocolate first as a bitter drink and only a thousand years later as the sweet solid confection we know today. The cocoa bean was first used by the Indian civilizations in South America to make a ceremonial drink and as currency for trade. The Aztecs called the drink "bitter water."

(TONE)

Q: What was one very early use of chocolate?

A. As a liquid medicine.
B. As a drink in ceremonies.
C. As a health drink mixed with sugar.
D. As a popular drink.

* bitter (ˈbɪtɚ) *adj.* 苦的　　solid (ˈsɑlɪd) *adj.* 固體的
confection (kənˈfɛkʃən) *n.* 糖果；甜點
ceremonial (ˌsɛrəˈmonɪəl) *adj.* 儀式的　　currency (ˈkɝənsɪ) *n.* 貨幣
trade (tred) *n.* 貿易　　liquid (ˈlɪkwɪd) *adj.* 液狀的

60. (**C**) Well, here's some news that may send you to the library.　The majority of Americans have not read a book in the last year. Six out of ten adults questioned said that the last time they could remember reading a book—other than the Bible—was a year ago or more.

(TONE)

Q: How many adults in the survey hadn't read any books other than the Bible in the past year or more?

A. About 6%.
B. About 16%.
C. About 60%.
D. About 66%.

* *six out of ten* 百分之六十　　*other than* 除了～之外
survey (ˈsɝve) *n.* 調查

English Listening Comprehension Test

Test Book No. 11

This listening comprehension test will test your ability to understand spoken English. In this test, each conversation, statement and question will be spoken JUST ONE TIME. They will not be written out for you. There are four parts to this test. Special instructions will be given to you at the beginning of each part.

Part A

In Part A, you will see several pictures in your test book. For each picture, you will be asked 1 to 3 questions. For each question, you will hear four possible answers. Choose the best answer according to what you see in the picture.

Example:

You will see:

You will hear: What is this?
A. This is a table.
B. This is a chair.
C. This is a watch.
D. This is a doll.

The best answer to the question "What is this?" is B: "This is a chair." Therefore, you should choose answer B.

A. Questions 1-2

D. Questions 9-10

B. Questions 3-6

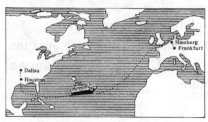

E. Questions 11-13

C. Questions 7-8

F. Questions 14-15

Part B

In Part B, you will hear 15 questions. After you hear a question, read the four possible answers in your test book and decide which one is the best answer to the question you have heard.

Example:

You will hear: What does your father do?

You will read: A. He's 50 years old.
B. He's a teacher.
C. He's hungry.
D. He's in Los Angeles.

The best answer to the question "What does your father do?" is B: "He's a teacher." Therefore, you should choose answer B.

Please go to the next page. ⇨

16. A. It doesn't matter.
    B. It's a serious matter.
    C. It's out of order.
    D. I don't like the matter.

17. A. Thank you very much.
    B. I'm so surprised!
    C. All right!
    D. She had a cold.

18. A. Thank you very much.
    B. Sure, I'll take it.
    C. Everything is on sale today.
    D. Not so good.

19. A. In junior high school.
    B. Three years.
    C. Yes, I have.
    D. Almost every day.

20. A. He's not there.
    B. He's working in his office.
    C. I thought he went fishing.
    D. I asked him to wait.

21. A. It leaves at 10:30.
    B. It is 10:30 now.
    C. It is very early.
    D. It is getting a little late.

22. A. I don't like to play cards.
    B. No, when were you there?
    C. Did you lend me a deck
       of cards?
    D. No cake for me, thanks.

23. A. I am ready.
    B. I have lost my watch.
    C. I am not wrong.
    D. I have finished my work.

24. A. No, I don't like them.
    B. Yes, they are delicious.
    C. I would like some tea.
    D. That costs a lot of money.

25. A. By train.
    B. About ten days.
    C. In one week.
    D. Five hours ago.

26. A. Today is our first day of
       business.
    B. No, I'll just look around.
    C. Anything you want.
    D. Here you are!

27. A. So can I.
    B. It is summer, you know.
    C. I left my jacket in your
       room.
    D. You caught a cold.

28. A. Why not tell the police
       officers?
    B. I have a new one.
    C. Would you lend me yours?
    D. I am so excited.

29. A. It's over there.
    B. He called me an hour ago.
    C. That was my friend, Tom.
    D. This is Allen speaking.

30. A. Neither.   She is a nurse.
    B. Yes, she is.
    C. No, she isn't.
    D. Either one will do.

Part C

In Part C, you will hear 15 conversations between a man and a woman. After each conversation, you will hear a question about the conversation. After you hear the question, read the four possible answers in your test book and choose the best answer to the question you have heard.

Example:

<u>You will hear</u>:　(Man)　　How do you go to school every day?
　　　　　　　　(Woman)　Usually by bus. Sometimes by taxi.

　　　　　　　　TONE:　　How does the woman go to school?

<u>You will read</u>:　A. She always goes to school on foot.
　　　　　　　　B. She usually takes a bike.
　　　　　　　　C. She takes either a bus or a taxi.
　　　　　　　　D. She usually goes to school by bus, never by taxi.

The best answer to the question "How does the woman go to school?" is C: "She takes either a bus or a taxi." Therefore, you should choose answer C.

Please go to the next page. ⇨

31. A. Political science.
    B. Economics.
    C. Getting an A.
    D. Political science and
       economics.

32. A. Changed her professor.
    B. Seen the professor.
    C. Changed her mind.
    D. Left school.

33. A. Her suitcase.
    B. Some rocks.
    C. The leaves.
    D. A down pillow.

34. A. Check the time of high tide.
    B. Go stand under the clock.
    C. Wait a little longer.
    D. Look for the traffic light.

35. A. Catch a cold.
    B. Hurry to catch the bus.
    C. Sit next to the bus stop.
    D. Fix his torn sleeve.

36. A. The room is on fire.
    B. They are bothered by the
       smoke.
    C. There is very little breeze.
    D. The men are not permitted
       in the room.

37. A. At a mine.
    B. In a new car showroom.
    C. In a parking lot.
    D. At a car repair shop.

38. A. They are both very tired
       of it.
    B. They are happy she's
       playing it at last.
    C. It is one of their favorite
       songs.
    D. They could listen to it
       another thousand times.

39. A. He's a boat builder.
    B. He smokes a pipe.
    C. He paints watercolors.
    D. He's a plumber.

40. A. A trip she has already
       taken.
    B. A trip she takes frequently.
    C. A restaurant she owns.
    D. A famous statue in
       Philadelphia.

41. A. Buying a new typewriter.
    B. Finding a new place for
       the typewriter.
    C. Finding a better typist.
    D. Questioning the typist.

42. A. Barry no longer lives in
       New York.
    B. Barry doesn't know how
       to economize.
    C. The woman called Barry
       in California.
    D. The woman didn't ever
       meet Barry.

43. A. Whether they should
       move west.
    B. A historical novel.
    C. Whether they once lived
       in the same town.
    D. A science course.

44. A. The ground is too hard for
       planting.
    B. Transportation is expensive
       from California.
    C. There has been too much
       rain in California.
    D. The planters are exper-
       imenting with new crops.

45. A. She was understanding.
    B. She was apologetic.
    C. She was annoyed.
    D. She was careless.

Part D

In Part D, you will hear 15 short talks.　After each talk, you will hear a question about the talk.　After you hear the question, read the four possible answers in your test book and choose the best answer to the question you have heard.

Example:

You will hear:　Well, that's all for Unit 15.　For today's homework, please do the review questions on page 80, and we'll check the answers tomorrow. Now, let's go on to Unit 16.

TONE:　What is the teacher going to do next in today's class?

You will read:　A. Check the homework.
　　　　　　　　B. Review Unit 15.
　　　　　　　　C. Start a new unit.
　　　　　　　　D. Answer students' questions.

The best answer to the question "What is the teacher going to do next in today's class?" is C: "Start a new unit."　Therefore, you should choose answer C.

Please go to the next page. ⇨

46. A. He has a part-time job.
　　B. He goes to the park with his friends.
　　C. He picks up his mother after work.
　　D. He takes care of his sister.

47. A. Japan.
　　B. Falling down a lot.
　　C. For the first time in his life.
　　D. Enjoying his time in the lodge.

48. A. The weather, museums, and parks are nice.
　　B. The cable cars stop at all the museums.
　　C. It's always filled with visitors.
　　D. All the big parks have museums.

49. A. Hawaii.
　　B. Okinawa.
　　C. Both Hawaii and Okinawa.
　　D. Neither Hawaii nor Okinawa.

50. A. In a public hall.
　　B. In a science museum.
　　C. In an examination hall.
　　D. In a university lecture hall.

51. A. People with digestion problems.
　　B. People with eating disorders.
　　C. People who want to try a new, effective diet.
　　D. People who have made themselves sick on various diets.

52. A. The adoption of a single global monetary unit.
　　B. Economic superpower status.
　　C. The installation of further trade barriers.
　　D. The exclusion of all other countries from its trading system.

53. A. The teaching of "shop" skills to only boys.
　　B. The teaching of home economics to only girls.
　　C. The teaching of "shop" skills to only girls.
　　D. The teaching of home economics to both sexes.

54. A. 6:30 a.m.
    B. 6:45 a.m.
    C. 11:30 a.m.
    D. 2:30 p.m.

55. A. Just after taking off in
       Miami.
    B. Just above the airport in
       Atlanta.
    C. Just after taking off in
       Jacksonville.
    D. Just above the St. Johns
       River.

56. A. In producing waste.
    B. In burning trash.
    C. In gaining weight.
    D. In driving cars.

57. A. A news item.
    B. An advertisement.
    C. A lecture.
    D. A tour description.

58. A. Someone was jealous of her.
    B. She was jealous of the
       murderer.
    C. She was a murderer.
    D. She committed suicide.

59. A. She killed them.
    B. She fed them.
    C. She rejected them.
    D. She rescued them.

60. A. It's about one-third.
    B. It's about half.
    C. It's about two-thirds.
    D. It's about the same.

Listening Test 11 詳解

Part A

For questions number 1 to 2, please look at picture A.

1. (**B**) Question number 1, what is the boy doing?
    A. He is going to bed.
    B. He is getting up.
    C. He is dreaming.
    D. He is exercising.

2. (**A**) Question number 2, please look at picture A again. What can be seen from the window?
    A. Mountains and trees can be seen.
    B. Mountains and the moon can be seen.
    C. A clock and a cat can be seen.
    D. A bird and a cat can be seen.

For questions number 3 to 6, please look at picture B.

3. (**B**) Question number 3, what is this?
    A. It is an atlas.
    B. It is a map.
    C. It is a globe.
    D. It is a model.

    * atlas (ˊætləs) *n.* 地圖集   globe (glob) *n.* 地球儀
    model (ˊmɑdl) *n.* 模型

4. (**C**) Question number 4, please look at picture B again. What is the dotted line?
    A. It is a coastline.
    B. It is the ship's road.
    C. It is the ship's route.
    D. It is North America.

    * *dotted line* 點狀線   route (rut) *n.* 路線

5. (**D**) Question number 5, please look at picture B again. Where is Dallas?
   A. It is on an island.
   B. It is in Europe.
   C. It is on the ship.
   D. It is in America.

6. (**D**) Question number 6, please look at picture B again. Where is the ship going?
   A. It is going to Dallas.
   B. It is going to North America.
   C. It is going to Africa.
   D. It is going to Europe.

For questions number 7 to 8, please look at picture C.

7. (**A**) Question number 7, what is the lady wearing?
   A. She is wearing a hat.
   B. She is wearing a vest.
   C. She is wearing glasses.
   D. She is wearing a miniskirt.

8. (**C**) Question number 8, please look at picture C again. What is the man doing?
   A. He is staring at the signal beside him.
   B. He is walking on the sidewalk.
   C. He is standing on the street near the corner by the crosswalk.
   D. He is trying to talk to the woman.

   * crosswalk〔'krɔs,wɔk〕*n.* 行人穿越道

For questions number 9 to 10, please look at picture D.

9. (**D**) Question number 9, where is the woman?
　　　　A. She is a mother of three kids.
　　　　B. She has her hands full.
　　　　C. She is at the gate of a supermarket.
　　　　D. She is at the door of her house.
　　　　* *have one's hands full* （某人）工作很忙

10. (**B**) Question number 10, please look at picture D again.　What is she going to do next?
　　　　A. She is going to lock the door.
　　　　B. She is going to open the door.
　　　　C. She is going to walk down the stairs.
　　　　D. She is going to throw away the food.

For questions number 11 to 13, please look at picture E.

11. (**B**) Question number 11, what is this a picture of?
　　　　A. It is a mall.
　　　　B. It is a market.
　　　　C. It is a piano bar.
　　　　D. It is a movie theater.
　　　　* bar (bɑr) *n.* 酒吧

12. (**C**) Question number 12, please look at picture E again.　What does the girl want?
　　　　A. She wants some fish.
　　　　B. She wants some milk.
　　　　C. She wants some fruit.
　　　　D. She wants some meat.

13. (**A**) Question number 13, please look at picture E again.　What is the girl carrying?
  A. She is carrying a basket.
  B. She is carrying a baby.
  C. She is carrying a vase.
  D. She is carrying a ball.
  * vase〔ves〕*n.* 花瓶

For questions number 14 to 15, please look at picture F.

14. (**D**) Question number 14, where are the people?
  A. They are in a lake.
  B. They are in a swimming pool.
  C. They are in a garden.
  D. They are in an office.

15. (**A**) Question number 15, please look at picture F again.　What is the man on the right doing?
  A. He is busy carrying papers.
  B. He is talking on the phone.
  C. He is talking to the other man.
  D. He is reading newspapers.

Part B

16. (**C**) What's wrong with your bike?
  A. It doesn't matter.
  B. It's a serious matter.
  C. It's out of order.
  D. I don't like the matter.
  * *out of order* 故障

17. (**D**) What happened to your sister?
    A. Thank you very much.
    B. I'm so surprised!
    C. All right!
    D. She had a cold.

18. (**D**) How is everything, Bill?
    A. Thank you very much.
    B. Sure, I'll take it.
    .C. Everything is on sale today.
    D. Not so good.

    * *on sale* 拍賣

19. (**B**) How long have you studied English?
    A. In junior high school.
    B. Three years.
    C. Yes, I have.
    D. Almost every day.

20. (**B**) Where is your father, John?
    A. He's not there.
    B. He's working in his office.
    C. I thought he went fishing.
    D. I asked him to wait.

21. (**A**) What time is your flight?
    A. It leaves at 10:30.
    B. It is 10:30 now.
    C. It is very early.
    D. It is getting a little late.

    * flight (flaɪt) *n.* 班機

22. (**B**) Did you get the card I sent from Bali?
    A. I don't like to play cards.
    B. No, when were you there?
    C. Did you lend me a deck of cards?
    D. No cake for me, thanks.

    * card (kɑrd) *n.* 明信片   Bali ('bɑlɪ) *n.* 巴里島
    deck (dɛk) *n.* 一副（牌）

23. (**B**) What's wrong, John?
    A. I am ready.
    B. I have lost my watch. ·
    C. I am not wrong.
    D. I have finished my work.

24. (**C**) Do you want tea or coffee?
    A. No, I don't like them.
    B. Yes, they are delicious.
    C. I would like some tea.
    D. That costs a lot of money.

25. (**C**) How soon is she coming back?
    A. By train.
    B. About ten days.
    C. In one week.
    D. Five hours ago.

26. (**B**) May I help you?
    A. Today is our first day of business.
    B. No, I'll just look around.
    C. Anything you want.
    D. Here you are!

27. (**B**) I can't believe it—another hot day.
    A. So can I.
    B. It is summer, you know.
    C. I left my jacket in your room.
    D. You caught a cold.

28. (**A**) My bicycle was lost.　What can I do now?
    A. Why not tell the police officers?
    B. I have a new one.
    C. Would you lend me yours?
    D. I am so excited.

29. (**C**) Who was that on the telephone?
    A. It's over there.
    B. He called me an hour ago.
    C. That was my friend, Tom.
    D. This is Allen speaking.

30. (**A**) Is Sue a doctor or a teacher?
    A. Neither.　She is a nurse.
    B. Yes, she is.
    C. No, she isn't.
    D. Either one will do.

Part C

31. (**B**) W: Rachael got an A in economics and only a C in political
    science.
    M: Well, I still say that political science is a little less
    complicated than economics.

(TONE)

Q: Which subject does the man think is harder?

A. Political science.

B. Economics.

C. Getting an A.

D. Political science and economics.

　* economics (͵ikə'nɑmɪks) *n.* 經濟學　***political science*** 政治學

32. (**C**)　M: Henry says this professor is very strict.

　　W: I used to believe that, too, but now I know it's untrue.

(TONE)

Q: What has the woman done recently?

A. Changed her professor.

B. Seen the professor.

C. Changed her mind.

D. Left school.

　* strict (strɪkt) *adj.* 嚴格的

33. (**A**)　W: I'm ready to leave now.　Will you bring down my suitcase?

　　M: Sure.　It certainly is heavy.　Are you carrying rocks?

(TONE)

Q: What did the woman want?

A. Her suitcase.　　　　　B. Some rocks.

C. The leaves.　　　　　　D. A down pillow.

　* suitcase ('sut͵kes) *n.* 公事包　***down pillow*** 羽絨枕頭

34. (**C**)　M: I can't understand why my friend isn't here yet.　We
agreed to meet at 10:30.　It's almost 11:00.　Do you think
we should try to call her, or go look for her?

　　W: She probably just got tied up in traffic.　Let's give her a
few more minutes.

(TONE)

Q: What are these people going to do?

A. Check the time of high tide.

B. Go stand under the clock.

C. Wait a little longer.

D. Look for the traffic light.

* **get tied up** 受阻　　**high tide** 高鋒（潮）

35. (**B**) M: Can you tell me when the next bus leaves for Bloomington?
W: The next bus leaves in three minutes.　If you run, you might catch it.

(TONE)

Q: What will the man probably do?

A. Catch a cold.

B. Hurry to catch the bus.

C. Sit next to the bus stop.

D. Fix his torn sleeve.

* **leave for** 前往　　sleeve〔 sliv 〕 n. 袖子

36. (**B**) W: This room is filled with smoke; I can hardly breathe.
M: I agree.　Smoking should not be permitted in this room at all.

(TONE)

Q: What can be concluded from this conversation?

A. The room is on fire.

B. They are bothered by the smoke.

C. There is very little breeze.

D. The men are not permitted in the room.

* breeze〔 briz 〕 n. 微風

37. (**D**) W: Could you have my car ready at 5:00 please?
　　　　M: Sure.　The damage is minor.

　　　　(TONE)
　　　　Q: Where did this conversation probably take place?
　　　　A. At a mine.
　　　　B. In a new car showroom.
　　　　C. In a parking lot.
　　　　D. At a car repair shop.

　　　* minor ('maɪnə) *adj.* 不嚴重的　　mine (maɪn) *n.* 礦坑
　　　　new car showroom 新車展示間　　**repair shop** 修理店

38. (**A**) W: I wish Mary would put on a different record.　She has
　　　　　　played that song a thousand times.
　　　　M: At least.　It used to be one of my favorites before I had to
　　　　　　hear it so often.

　　　　(TONE)
　　　　Q: What do the man and woman say about Mary's record?
　　　　A. They are both very tired of it.
　　　　B. They are happy she's playing it at last.
　　　　C. It is one of their favorite songs.
　　　　D. They could listen to it another thousand times.

　　　* *put on* 播放

39. (**D**) W: The pipe is leaking and there's water all over the floor.
　　　　M: Why don't you call Mr. Peters?

　　　　(TONE)
　　　　Q: What does Mr. Peters do?
　　　　A. He's a boat builder.　　　　B. He smokes a pipe.
　　　　C. He paints watercolors.　　　D. He's a plumber.

　　　* pipe (paɪp) *n.* 管子　　leak (lik) *v.* 漏 (水)
　　　　watercolor ('wɔtə,kʌləz) *n.* 水彩　　plumber ('plʌmə) *n.* 水管工人

40. (**A**)　M: Tell me about your trip to Philadelphia.
　　　　　W: Well, we walked a lot, visited some interesting monuments,
　　　　　　　and finished up at a good restaurant.

　　　　　(TONE)
　　　　　Q: What is the woman talking about?
　　　　　A. A trip she has already taken.
　　　　　B. A trip she takes frequently.
　　　　　C. A restaurant she owns.
　　　　　D. A famous statue in Philadelphia.

　　　　　* Philadelphia (,fɪlə'dɛlfjə) *n.* 費城
　　　　　　monument ('mɑnjəmənt) *n.* 紀念館　　statue ('stætʃu) *n.* 雕像

41. (**C**)　M: I think we should replace that old typewriter.
　　　　　W: Why not the typist?

　　　　　(TONE)
　　　　　Q: What did the woman suggest?
　　　　　A. Buying a new typewriter.
　　　　　B. Finding a new place for the typewriter.
　　　　　C. Finding a better typist.
　　　　　D. Questioning the typist.

42. (**A**)　M: I went to New York yesterday, but I forgot to call Barry.
　　　　　W: Barry wouldn't have been there anyway.　He's an
　　　　　　　economist in California now.

　　　　　(TONE)
　　　　　Q: What information does the man find out?
　　　　　A. Barry no longer lives in New York.
　　　　　B. Barry doesn't know how to economize.
　　　　　C. The woman called Barry in California.
　　　　　D. The woman didn't ever meet Barry.

　　　　　* economist (ɪ'kɑnəmɪst) *n.* 經濟學者
　　　　　　economize (ɪ'kɑnə,maɪz) *v.* 節約

43. (**B**) W: I've been reading a fascinating book about life in the
old West.
M: I wonder if it's the same one I read last month.

(TONE)
Q: What are these people discussing?
A. Whether they should move west.
B. A historical novel.
C. Whether they once lived in the same town.
D. A science course.

* fascinating ('fæsn͵etɪŋ) *adj.* 很棒的

44. (**C**) M: This year's heavy rainfall has caused flooding, and made it
hard to plant new crops in California.
W: Yes. I guess that's why fruit and vegetables are so expensive
right now.

(TONE)
Q: What is the problem?
A. The ground is too hard for planting.
B. Transportation is expensive from California.
C. There has been too much rain in California.
D. The planters are experimenting with new crops.

* rainfall ('ren͵fɔl) *n.* 降雨   flooding ('flʌdɪŋ) *n.* 淹水；氾濫

45. (**C**) M: I hope you can understand my reasons for deciding to
leave, Mrs. Harrison.
W: Do I have to remind you that we have invested a lot of
time and money in your career here?

(TONE)
Q: How did Mrs. Harrison respond?
A. She was understanding.   B. She was apologetic.
C. She was annoyed.   D. She was careless.

* apologetic (ə͵pɑlə'dʒɛtɪk) *adj.* 道歉的

Part D

46. (**D**) Bill is a high school student, and his sister Nancy is six years old. Their mother works in the afternoon, so Bill picks up Nancy after school. They often go to the park and play for an hour before going home.

(TONE)
Q: What does Bill do in the afternoon?
A. He has a part-time job.
B. He goes to the park with his friends.
C. He picks up his mother after work.
D. He takes care of his sister.

* *pick up* 順道去接~

47. (**D**) Mike went to Japan with his friends last winter. Then he tried skiing for the first time in his life. The first day, he fell down again and again, so he was very tired. The next day, he read some books in the lodge, and watched the snowy landscape from the window. He liked this part of the ski trip the best.

(TONE)
Q: What was Mike's favorite part of the ski trip?
A. Japan.
B. Falling down a lot.
C. For the first time in his life.
D. Enjoying his time in the lodge.

* lodge (lɑdʒ) *n.* 山林小屋　　landscape (ˈlænd͵skep) *n.* 風景

48. (**A**) San Francisco is one of the best tourist spots in the United States. The weather is nice all year, and there are many fun places to go. People often get around the city by cable car. The parks and museums are beautiful and always filled with visitors.

(TONE)

Q: Why is San Francisco so popular with tourists?

A. The weather, museums, and parks are nice.

B. The cable cars stop at all the museums.

C. It's always filled with visitors.

D. All the big parks have museums.

* *tourist spot* 觀光點　　*cable car* 電纜車

49. (**A**) Tom and his friends have decided to go on a trip before they graduate from college. Tom wants to go to Okinawa, but his friends say they want to visit Hawaii. Tom will probably have to agree with his friends.

(TONE)

Q: Where are Tom and his friends most likely to visit?

A. Hawaii.　　　　　　　　B. Okinawa.

C. Both Hawaii and Okinawa.

D. Neither Hawaii nor Okinawa.

* Okinawa (okɪ'nɑwə) *n.* 沖繩縣 (隸屬日本)

50. (**D**) The subject we shall be looking at today is volcanoes. In the first part of my lecture I'm going to talk about what volcanoes are and how they're formed. Later I shall be discussing some specific well-known volcanoes. I recommend that you take detailed notes, as you're going to be tested on this subject in the midterm exam.

(TONE)

Q: Where is the speaker?

A. In a public hall.　　　　B. In a science museum.

C. In an examination hall.　D. In a university lecture hall.

* volcano (vɑl'keno) *n.* 火山　　lecture ('lɛktʃɚ) *n.* 授課
  specific (spɪ'sɪfɪk) *adj.* 特定的　　detailed ('di'teld) *adj.* 詳細的
  midterm exam 期中考　　*lecture hall* 課堂

51. (**B**) Are you overweight yet unable to satisfy your craving for food?
Are you sick of trying endless ineffective diets, or unable to
stay on a diet for more than a couple of days? If you have a
problem controlling the amount you eat, whether it's a new
problem or one that just won't go away, Gluttons Unlimited
want to hear from you.

(TONE)
Q: At what kind of people is this advertisement aimed?
A. People with digestion problems.
B. People with eating disorders.
C. People who want to try a new, effective diet.
D. People who have made themselves sick on various diets.

 * overweight (ˈovɚˌwet) adj. 過重的　　*crave for* 渴望～
 on a diet 節食　　glutton (ˈglʌtn̩) n. 暴食者
 eating disorder 飲食失調

52. (**B**) By the year 2020, the EC will be the most powerful trading
bloc in the world. The advent of a single monetary unit,
plus the lowering of trade barriers, will inspire speculative
investment from within Europe.

(TONE)
Q: What will the EC have achieved by the year 2020?
A. The adoption of a single global monetary unit.
B. Economic superpower status.
C. The installation of further trade barriers.
D. The exclusion of all other countries from its trading system.

 * *EC* 歐洲共同體 (= *European Community*)
 trading bloc 貿易聯盟　　advent (ˈædvɛnt) n. 出現
 monetary unit 貨幣單元　　*trade barrier* 貿易障礙
 inspire (ɪnˈspaɪr) v. 促進
 speculative (ˈspɛkjəˌletɪv) adj. 投機性的
 installation (ˌɪnstəˈleʃən) n. 安裝

53. (**D**) I support the recent trend in high schools toward teaching home economics skills to both girls and boys. Traditionally, girls received instruction in home economics, while boys were taught carpentry or mechanical skills, commonly known as "shop." As all of these skills are very practical and useful, it is unwise to restrict access to them based on the gender of a student.

(TONE)

Q: What current trend does the speaker support?

A. The teaching of "shop" skills to only boys.

B. The teaching of home economics to only girls.

C. The teaching of "shop" skills to only girls.

D. The teaching of home economics to both sexes.

   * trend〔trɛnd〕*n.* 趨勢　　***home economics skill*** 家庭理財技術
     instruction〔ɪn'strʌkʃən〕*n.* 教育
     carpentry〔'kɑrpəntrɪ〕*n.* 木工　　shop〔ʃɑp〕*n.* 工藝
     gender〔'dʒɛndɚ〕*n.* 性別

54. (**A**) Good morning, and thank you for using the Bluehound Bus Service connecting all points between San Francisco and Seattle with safety and convenience. The San Francisco-Seattle express bus departs at 6:30 a.m., and for those passengers bound for Eugene, the San Francisco-Portland local bus leaves at 6:45 a.m.

(TONE)

Q: What time does the San Francisco-Seattle express bus depart?

A. 6:30 a.m.

B. 6:45 a.m.

C. 11:30 a.m.

D. 2:30 p.m.

   * ***express bus*** 快速公車　　***be bound for*** （準備）前往～的
     local bus 每站停的公車

55. (**D**) We flew from Miami along the coast of Florida, and right
before landing in Jacksonville, just above the St. Johns River,
the plane dipped sharply. As we were so close to the water,
I thought we were going to crash into the river. I'll tell you,
I was really glad to be on the ground again.

(TONE)
Q: Where did the plane dip sharply?
A. Just after taking off in Miami.
B. Just above the airport in Atlanta.
C. Just after taking off in Jacksonville.
D. Just above the St. Johns River.

* landing (ˈlændɪŋ) *n.* 降落   dip (dɪp) *v.* 下沈

56. (**A**) The U.S. leads the world in waste production. America
generates some 200 million tons a year, enough to fill a
convoy of garbage trucks stretching eight times around
the globe. Each American discards 3.6 pounds of trash a
day, almost twice as much as the average German does.

(TONE)
Q: In what way do Americans lead the world?
A. In producing waste.   B. In burning trash.
C. In gaining weight.   D. In driving cars.

* waste (west) *n.* 廢棄物   convoy (ˈkɑnvɔɪ) *n.* 車隊
stretch (strɛtʃ) *v.* 延伸   discard (dɪsˈkɑrd) *v.* 丟棄

57. (**B**) Our best material is taken from the best sheep of Scotland and
is carefully processed. Only the highest quality wool is used
in our products, thus making our excellent sweaters the best in
the world. If you want style and comfort, try our remarkable
"Super Comfort" line of clothing.

(TONE)

Q: What is this announcement?

A. A news item.　　　　　B. An advertisement.

C. A lecture.　　　　　　D. A tour description.

* material (məˈtɪrɪəl) *n.* 原料　　process (ˈprɑsɛs) *v.* 處理
remarkable (rɪˈmɑrkəbḷ) *adj.* 有名的　　item (ˈaɪtəm) *n.* 一則 (新聞)

58. (**A**) A young woman has been found murdered in her home. The means used was poison, and the motive appears to have been jealousy. This is the third case of poisoning in ten days.

(TONE)

Q: Why was the woman killed?

A. Someone was jealous of her.

B. She was jealous of the murderer.

C. She was a murderer.

D. She committed suicide.

* motive (ˈmotɪv) *n.* 動機　　jealousy (ˈdʒɛləsɪ) *n.* 嫉妒

59. (**C**) There was a problem at the zoo. Leopard cubs had just been born. As unfortunately so often happens with zoo animals, its mother seemed not to know what to do with them, and refused to feed them. So what was to be done? By a great piece of good fortune, a mongrel dog whose puppies had been stolen came to the rescue.

(TONE)

Q: What did the mother leopard do with her cubs?

A. She killed them.　　　　B. She fed them.

C. She rejected them.　　　D. She rescued them.

* leopard (ˈlɛpəd) *n.* 美洲豹　　cub (kʌb) *n.* 幼獸
by a great piece of good fortune 非常幸運地
mongrel (ˈmʌŋgrəl) *adj.* 雜種的　　puppy (ˈpʌpɪ) *n.* 小狗
come to the rescue 伸出援手

60. (**A**)　Have you decided where you want to live for your retirement?
　　　Here's one place you might want to consider.　Mexico.
　　　Recently, Mexico has been attracting increasing numbers of
　　　U.S. retirees.　It's not just romance—leaving the U.S. can be
　　　a way to stretch your retirement dollar.　Mexico offers the
　　　best bargains.　The cost of living there is only about one-third
　　　that of living in the U.S.

　　　(TONE)
　　　Q:　What is the cost of living in Mexico compared to the
　　　　　United States?
　　　A.　It's about one-third.
　　　B.　It's about half.
　　　C.　It's about two-thirds.
　　　D.　It's about the same.

　　　* retirement (rɪ'taɪrmənt) *n.* 退休　　retiree (rɪ,taɪ'ri) *n.* 退休人員
　　　cost of living 生活費

English Listening Comprehension Test

Test Book No. 12

This listening comprehension test will test your ability to understand spoken English. In this test, each conversation, statement and question will be spoken JUST ONE TIME. They will not be written out for you. There are four parts to this test. Special instructions will be given to you at the beginning of each part.

Part A

In Part A, you will see several pictures in your test book. For each picture, you will be asked 1 to 3 questions. For each question, you will hear four possible answers. Choose the best answer according to what you see in the picture.

Example:

<u>You will see:</u>

<u>You will hear:</u>   What is this?
A. This is a table.
B. This is a chair.
C. This is a watch.
D. This is a doll.

The best answer to the question "What is this?" is B: "This is a chair." Therefore, you should choose answer B.

A. Questions 1-3

B. Questions 4-6

C. Questions 7-9

D. Questions 10-12

E. Questions 13-15

Part B

In Part B, you will hear 15 questions. After you hear a question, read the four possible answers in your test book and decide which one is the best answer to the question you have heard.

Example:

<u>You will hear:</u>   What does your father do?

<u>You will read:</u>   A. He's 50 years old.
B. He's a teacher.
C. He's hungry.
D. He's in Los Angeles.

The best answer to the question "What does your father do?" is B: "He's a teacher." Therefore, you should choose answer B.

Please go to the next page. ⇨

16. A. To the park.
    B. In the office.
    C. Yes, they are walking home.
    D. On campus.

17. A. By bus.
    B. He didn't sleep.
    C. It is summer.
    D. I don't know.

18. A. It's very cold.
    B. It snowed a lot.
    C. It usually snows.
    D. It was quite hot.

19. A. How much does one cost?
    B. How many do you need?
    C. How do I spend my money?
    D. How much money do I have?

20. A. I have a new watch.
    B. You can go by taxi.
    C. About twenty minutes.
    D. What time is it?

21. A. It's time to go.
    B. I hope so!
    C. So did I.
    D. Come in, John.

22. A. I've thought about it.
    B. I've done many of them.
    C. No. Can you help me
       with it?
    D. Yes, I have done them.

23. A. I can't believe it.
    B. I can't wait.
    C. Did you hear that?
    D. Yes, I know.

24. A. It never stays right here.
    B. It's right across the street.
    C. It goes to the park.
    D. They stop to take a bus.

25. A. Can I help you?
    B. Bring me a towel, please.
    C. I'll do anything I can.
    D. How can you do that?

26. A. It takes time.
    B. Do you want something
       to eat?
    C. Be careful.
    D. I'll get one for you.

27. A. I am at school.
    B. I am going to school.
    C. I am a student.
    D. I am doing my homework.

28. A. Yes, I don't have anything
       to do this afternoon.
    B. Can you go with me?
    C. I don't know yet.
    D. I did a lot of work this
       afternoon.

29. A. Of course, I am.
    B. Of course, I do.
    C. Who is that man?
    D. Who said that?

30. A. No, I never did that before.
    B. No, I never saw one before.
    C. Yes, I never did.
    D. No, I sometimes did.

Part C

In Part C, you will hear 15 conversations between a man and a woman.　After each conversation, you will hear a question about the conversation.　After you hear the question, read the four possible answers in your test book and choose the best answer to the question you have heard.

Example:

You will hear:　(Man)　　How do you go to school every day?
　　　　　　　 (Woman)　 Usually by bus.　Sometimes by taxi.

　　　　　　　 TONE:　　 How does the woman go to school?

You will read:　A. She always goes to school on foot.
　　　　　　　　 B. She usually takes a bike.
　　　　　　　　 C. She takes either a bus or a taxi.
　　　　　　　　 D. She usually goes to school by bus, never by
　　　　　　　　　　 taxi.

The best answer to the question "How does the woman go to school?" is C: "She takes either a bus or a taxi."　Therefore, you should choose answer C.

Please go to the next page. ⇨

31. A. A visitor has borrowed it.
    B. She had given it to her guide.
    C. A friend took it to the West.
    D. Bill gave it back to his friend.

32. A. In a drugstore.
    B. In a hardware store.
    C. In a snack bar.
    D. In a bakery.

33. A. Picking up ice cubes.
    B. Betting all forty dollars.
    C. Leaving in forty minutes.
    D. Leaving immediately.

34. A. Feeling sorry for himself.
    B. Asking for change.
    C. Trying to purchase two pickles.
    D. Sending a package.

35. A. One.
    B. Two.
    C. Three.
    D. Six.

36. A. It has a lot of students in it.
    B. It's going to be a lot of fun.
    C. It's going to require a lot of reading.
    D. It seems to be working out quite well.

37. A. The new driveway has been completed.
    B. The store was damaged.
    C. The work wasn't properly done.
    D. The area is flooded after the rain.

38. A. She was unsure of how Jill really felt.
    B. She didn't like it.
    C. She was excited about it.
    D. She was sure she wouldn't use it.

39. A. Use the back door.
    B. Fail to deliver his package.
    C. See a different person.
    D. Act in front of an audience.

40. A. He surprised the woman during dinner.
    B. He went to exactly two shops.
    C. He bought something that wasn't on the list.
    D. He brought home someone she wasn't expecting.

41. A. Where to have her shoes fixed.
    B. What the latest scandal was.
    C. How to get to the other side of the intersection.
    D. Which section of town is best for shopping.

42. A. The director spoke too long.
    B. The actors were not very good.
    C. It was difficult to follow the action.
    D. There was too little action.

43. A. It's time for his eye drops.
    B. He should clean up what he dropped.
    C. He should pour more water in the glasses.
    D. It's perfectly clear outside.

44. A. Apply for the fellowship.
    B. Take a statistics course.
    C. Check her background research.
    D. Pick a more opportune moment.

45. A. They've been working at the telescope for two days.
    B. They can't find the microscope.
    C. They've been working in the laboratory for two hours.
    D. They can't fix the microphone.

Part D

In Part D, you will hear 15 short talks. After each talk, you will hear a question about the talk. After you hear the question, read the four possible answers in your test book and choose the best answer to the question you have heard.

Example:

<u>You will hear:</u>   Well, that's all for Unit 15. For today's homework, please do the review questions on page 80, and we'll check the answers tomorrow. Now, let's go on to Unit 16.

TONE: What is the teacher going to do next in today's class?

<u>You will read:</u>   A. Check the homework.
B. Review Unit 15.
C. Start a new unit.
D. Answer students' questions.

The best answer to the question "What is the teacher going to do next in today's class?" is C: "Start a new unit."   Therefore, you should choose answer C.

Please go to the next page. ⇨

46. A. Take a cooking class.
    B. Have dinner at home.
    C. Go to Mexico.
    D. Go out to a Mexican restaurant.

47. A. Studied biographies.
    B. Kept busy.
    C. Visited his parents.
    D. Worked in a restaurant.

48. A. Tama is the cutest cat.
    B. Tama sleeps with her.
    C. Tama is the youngest cat.
    D. Tama wakes her up.

49. A. The front page.
    B. The sports page.
    C. The comics.
    D. The business section.

50. A. He works for a hotel.
    B. He works for a transport company.
    C. He works in reception.
    D. He's a telephone engineer.

51. A. Morning.
    B. Afternoon.
    C. Night.
    D. It's impossible to tell.

52. A. 11:00.
    B. A quarter to five.
    C. 11:45.
    D. At four or five.

53. A. People who use a credit card a lot.
    B. People who make many monthly payments by check.
    C. People who have a large amount of money.
    D. People who need to start saving.

54. A. It catches only target fish.
    B. It is smaller.
    C. It is indiscriminate in what it catches.
    D. It is used only in the Pacific Ocean.

55. A. From 9:00 a.m. to 8:00 p.m.
    B. From 9:00 a.m. to 9:00 p.m.
    C. From 9:00 a.m. to midnight.
    D. From noon to 9:00 p.m.

56. A. Today's meeting.
    B. Additional meetings.
    C. Future farm subsidies.
    D. Yesterday's agreement.

57. A. An examiner.
    B. A taxi driver.
    C. A school teacher.
    D. A banker.

58. A. In an airport.
    B. At a port.
    C. In a city office.
    D. At a train station.

59. A. A first-class train ride all the way across Europe.
    B. Only three days of train travel among major European capitals.
    C. A whole month's unlimited second-class train travel.
    D. A two-month uninterrupted trip by train.

60. A. They sometimes get anxious and depressed.
    B. They usually need to see a doctor to receive medication.
    C. They don't develop symptoms at first.
    D. They feel worse when they return to coffee drinking.

Listening Test 12 詳解

Part A

For questions number 1 to 3, please look at picture A.

1. (**D**) Question number 1, what season is it?
   A. It is spring.
   B. It is summer.
   C. It is autumn.
   D. It is winter.

2. (**B**) Question number 2, please look at picture A again. What is the man on the right doing?
   A. He is walking.
   B. He is jogging.
   C. He is skating.
   D. He is swimming.
   * skate (sket) v. 溜冰

3. (**C**) Question number 3, please look at picture A again. What are the couple on the left doing?
   A. They are jogging.
   B. They are walking a dog.
   C. They are chasing a bus.
   D. They are looking for a tube of toothpaste.
   * ***walk a dog*** 遛狗   chase (tʃes) v. 追
      tube (tjub) n. 管狀物   toothpaste (ˈtuθ͵pest) n. 牙膏

For questions number 4 to 6, please look at picture B.

4. (**B**) Question number 4, what are the children doing?
   A. They are shopping.
   B. They are playing a game.
   C. They are fighting.
   D. They are taking a test.

5. (**C**) Question number 5, please look at picture B again.　What are they wearing?
   A. They are wearing T-shirts.
   B. They are wearing dresses.
   C. They are wearing blindfolds.
   D. They are wearing glasses.
   * blindfold (ˈblaɪnd,fold) *n.* 眼罩

6. (**D**) Question number 6, please look at picture B again.　What is the boy holding?
   A. He is holding a shirt.
   B. He is holding a pot.
   C. He is holding a can.
   D. He is holding a bottle.
   * pot (pɑt) *n.* 茶壺　　can (kæn) *n.* 罐頭

For questions number 7 to 9, please look at picture C.

7. (**D**) Question number 7, what are the girls doing?
   A. They are watching TV.
   B. They are singing.
   C. They are studying.
   D. They are fighting.
   * fight (faɪt) *v.* 爭吵

8. (**A**) Question number 8, please look at picture C again.　How many dolls are there?
   A. There are three dolls.
   B. There are four dolls.
   C. There are six dolls.
   D. There are eleven dolls.

9. (**C**) Question number 9, please look at picture C again.　Where are the dogs?

    A. They are on the bed.

    B. They are on the bookcase.

    C. They are on the armchairs.

    D. They are on the floor.

    * bookcase (ˈbʊkˌkes) *n.* 書架　　armchair (ˈɑrmˌtʃɛr) *n.* 扶手椅

For questions number 10 to 12, please look at picture D.

10. (**D**) Question number 10, what place is this?

    A. This is a bank.

    B. This is a train station.

    C. This is a hotel.

    D. This is an airport.

11. (**C**) Question number 11, please look at picture D again.　What section of the airport is this?

    A. This is a check-in counter.

    B. This is a departure hall.

    C. This is a baggage claim area.

    D. This is a lost and found.

    * *check-in counter* 辦理登記手續的櫃台　　*departure hall* 離境大廳
    baggage claim area 行李提領處　　*lost and found* 失物招領處

12. (**D**) Question number 12, please look at picture D again.　Who is "E"?

    A. He is Mr. Johnson.

    B. He is Mr. Johnson's wife.

    C. He is a worker in the airport.

    D. He is Mr. Johnson's guide.

    * guide (gaɪd) *n.* 導遊

For questions number 13 to 15, please look at picture E.

13. (**C**) Question number 13, what is this a picture of?
    A. This is an elementary school.
    B. This is a kindergarten.
    C. This is a day-care center.
    D. This is a picture of a hospital.
    * *day-care center* 托兒所

14. (**B**) Question number 14, please look at picture E again.　What is "B" doing?
    A. She is changing the baby's dress.
    B. She is changing the baby's diapers.
    C. She is feeding the baby.
    D. She is bathing the baby.
    * diaper (ˈdaɪəpɚ) *n.* 尿布　　bathe (beð) *v.* 給~洗澡

15. (**B**) Question number 15, please look at picture E again.　Where is "G" sleeping?
    A. He is sleeping in a bunk bed.
    B. He is sleeping in a crib.
    C. He is sleeping in a cradle.
    D. He is sleeping in a sofa bed.
    * *bunk bed* 上下舖　　crib (krɪb) *n.* 嬰兒床
    cradle (ˈkrædḷ) *n.* 搖籃　*sofa bed* 沙發床

Part B

16. (**A**) Where are you going?
    A. To the park.
    B. In the office.
    C. Yes, they are walking home.
    D. On campus.
    * *on campus* 在校園裏

17. (**D**) Who will go with him?

    A. By bus.   B. He didn't sleep.

    C. It is summer.   D. I don't know.

18. (**B**) What was the weather like in New York last winter?

    A. It's very cold.

    B. It snowed a lot.

    C. It usually snows.

    D. It was quite hot.

19. (**A**) Good evening. We are having a special sale on sweaters today.

    A. How much does one cost?

    B. How many do you need?

    C. How do I spend my money?

    D. How much money do I have?

20. (**C**) How long is it to the next town?

    A. I have a new watch.

    B. You can go by taxi.

    C. About twenty minutes.

    D. What time is it?

21. (**B**) We'll catch a lot of fish.

    A. It's time to go.   B. I hope so!

    C. So did I.   D. Come in, John.

22. (**C**) Have you done your homework, Joe?

    A. I've thought about it.

    B. I've done many of them.

    C. No. Can you help me with it?

    D. Yes, I have done them.

    * homework 「家庭作業」爲不可數名詞。

23. (**B**)　We'll visit Mr. Wang's farm.　There's lots of fruit there.
　　　　A.　I can't believe it.
　　　　B.　I can't wait.
　　　　C.　Did you hear that?
　　　　D.　Yes, I know.

24. (**B**)　Where is the bus stop?
　　　　A.　It never stays right here.
　　　　B.　It's right across the street.
　　　　C.　It goes to the park.
　　　　D.　They stop to take a bus.
　　　　* *across the street* 在對街　　*bus stop* 公車站牌

25. (**C**)　I want you to do me a favor.
　　　　A.　Can I help you?
　　　　B.　Bring me a towel, please.
　　　　C.　I'll do anything I can.
　　　　D.　How can you do that?
　　　　* towel ('tauəl) *n.* 毛巾

26. (**D**)　I'd like a Coke.
　　　　A.　It takes time.
　　　　B.　Do you want something to eat?
　　　　C.　Be careful.
　　　　D.　I'll get one for you.

27. (**B**)　Where are you going?
　　　　A.　I am at school.
　　　　B.　I am going to school.
　　　　C.　I am a student.
　　　　D.　I am doing my homework.

28. (**C**) What are you going to do this afternoon?
    A. Yes, I don't have anything to do this afternoon.
    B. Can you go with me?
    C. I don't know yet.
    D. I did a lot of work this afternoon.

29. (**B**) Don't you understand John's speech?
    A. Of course, I am.
    B. Of course, I do.
    C. Who is that man?
    D. Who said that?

30. (**A**) Did you ever talk to an American?
    A. No, I never did that before.
    B. No, I never saw one before.
    C. Yes, I never did.
    D. No, I sometimes did.

Part C

31. (**A**) W: Have you seen my guide to wild birds anywhere, Bill?
    M: Oh, yes. I lent it to a guest, but I thought he had given it back already.

    (TONE)
    Q: Why can't the woman find her book?
    A. A visitor has borrowed it.
    B. She had given it to her guide.
    C. A friend took it to the West.
    D. Bill gave it back to his friend.

    * guide (gaɪd) *n.* 指南；簡介 (= *guidebook*)

32. (**A**) W: Can I help you, please?

M: I want to have this prescription filled and a bottle of aspirin.

(TONE)

Q: Where did this conversation take place?

A. In a drugstore. 　　B. In a hardware store.

C. In a snack bar. 　　D. In a bakery.

* *fill the prescription* 按處方配藥　　aspirin (ˈæspərɪn) *n.* 阿斯匹靈

drugstore (ˈdrʌg͵stor) *n.* 藥房　　*hardware store* 五金行

33. (**D**) M: Why don't we have a drink first?　We still have 40 minutes.

W: No.　We don't, we'd better get moving.

(TONE)

Q: What does the woman suggest?

A. Picking up ice cubes.

B. Betting all forty dollars.

C. Leaving in forty minutes.

D. Leaving immediately.

* *ice cube* 冰塊　　bet (bɛt) *v.* 賭 (錢)

34. (**B**) M: Do you have two nickels for a dime?

W: I don't even have a cent.

(TONE)

Q: What does the man suggest?

A. Feeling sorry for himself.

B. Asking for change.

C. Trying to purchase two pickles.

D. Sending a package.

* nickel (ˈnɪkl̩) *n.* 五分錢　　dime (daɪm) *n.* 十分錢

change (tʃendʒ) *n.* 零錢　　purchase (ˈpɜtʃəs) *v.* 購買

pickle (ˈpɪkl̩) *n.* 酸黃瓜

35. (**B**) W: Good morning, may I please have one adult and 2 children?
　　　　　M: Here are 2 tickets for you and your older boy.　Children
　　　　　under six are free.

　　　　　(TONE)
　　　　　Q: How many tickets does the woman have to buy?
　　　　　A. One.　　　　　　　　B. Two.
　　　　　C. Three.　　　　　　　D. Six.

　　　　　* free〔 fri 〕*adj.* 免費的

36. (**C**) W: It looks like the English course is going to be a lot of work.
　　　　　M: Didn't you see the reading list is enormous?

　　　　　(TONE)
　　　　　Q: What did they think of the English course?
　　　　　A. It has a lot of students in it.
　　　　　B. It's going to be a lot of fun.
　　　　　C. It's going to require a lot of reading.
　　　　　D. It seems to be working out quite well.

　　　　　* enormous〔 ɪˋnɔrməs 〕*adj.* 巨大的　　***work out*** 順利進行

37. (**D**) M: The storm did a lot of damage to my property.
　　　　　W: It did to mine, too.　My lawn is completely under water.

　　　　　(TONE)
　　　　　Q: What happened?
　　　　　A. The new driveway has been completed.
　　　　　B. The store was damaged.
　　　　　C. The work wasn't properly done.
　　　　　D. The area is flooded after the rain.

　　　　　* property〔ˋprɑpətɪ〕*n.* 財產　　　lawn〔 lɔn 〕*n.* 草地
　　　　　driveway〔ˋdraɪv͵we 〕*n.* 私人車道　　flood〔 flʌd 〕*v.* 淹水

38. (**A**) W: I couldn't tell if Jill liked the idea or she was only being polite.
M: Oh, I'm sure she wouldn't have been so enthusiastic about it if she didn't like it.

(TONE)
Q: How does the woman feel about Jill?
A. She was unsure of how Jill really felt.
B. She didn't like it.
C. She was excited about it.
D. She was sure she wouldn't use it.

* enthusiastic (ɪn,θjuzɪ'æstɪk) *adj.* 熱心的

39. (**A**) W: What is he doing at the back door?
M: They say people delivering the packages shouldn't use the front door.

(TONE)
Q: What should the deliveryman do?
A. Use the back door.
B. Fail to deliver his package.
C. See a different person.
D. Act in front of an audience.

* deliveryman (dɪ'lɪvɚɪ,mæn) *n.* 送貨員　　*fail to* 無法

40. (**C**) W: Did you get the things on the shopping list?
M: Not exactly. I bought something special, a surprise for dinner.

(TONE)
Q: What did the man do?
A. He surprised the woman during dinner.
B. He went to exactly two shops.
C. He bought something that wasn't on the list.
D. He brought home someone she wasn't expecting.

* *shopping list* 購物清單

41. (**A**) W: Do you know where I can get my sandals fixed?
　　　　 M: There's a shoe repair shop on the other side of the intersection.

　　　　 (TONE)
　　　　 Q: What does the woman want to know?
　　　　 A. Where to have her shoes fixed.
　　　　 B. What the latest scandal was.
　　　　 C. How to get to the other side of the intersection.
　　　　 D. Which section of town is best for shopping.
　　　　 * sandal ('sændl̩) n. 涼鞋　　 intersection (ˌɪntə'sɛkʃən) n. 十字路口

42. (**D**) W: What did you think of the play?
　　　　 M: It was well acted and directed, but I don't like plays that
　　　　　　 are all words and not much action.

　　　　 (TONE)
　　　　 Q: What was the man's opinion of the play?
　　　　 A. The director spoke too long.
　　　　 B. The actors were not very good.
　　　　 C. It was difficult to follow the action.
　　　　 D. There was too little action.
　　　　 * play (ple) n. 戲劇　　 director (də'rɛktə) n. 導演

43. (**D**) M: Look, it's pouring outside.
　　　　 W: I think you need to clean your glasses. There isn't a drop
　　　　　　 in the sky.

　　　　 (TONE)
　　　　 Q: What does the woman say to the man?
　　　　 A. It's time for his eye drops.
　　　　 B. He should clean up what he dropped.
　　　　 C. He should pour more water in the glasses.
　　　　 D. It's perfectly clear outside.
　　　　 * pour (por) v. 下傾盆大雨　　 *eye drops* 眼藥水

44. (**A**) M: Did you see the bulletin put up by the fellowship committee? It's offering support for advanced work specializing in Scandinavian population studies. With your background you should take advantage of this opportunity.

W: My research does fit the description, so maybe I will apply for it.

(TONE)

Q: What does the man think the woman should do?

A. Apply for the fellowship.
B. Take a statistics course.
C. Check her background research.
D. Pick a more opportune moment.

* bulletin ('bulətɪn) *n.* 公告　***put up***　張貼
fellowship ('fɛlo,ʃɪp) *n.* (研究生) 獎學金
specialize in 專攻　statistics (stə'tɪstɪks) *n.* 統計學
opportune (,ɑpɚ'tjun) *adj.* 適當的

45. (**C**) W: I think we should take a break. We've been working here for 2 hours.

M: I'd be glad to. I've been looking through this microscope for 2 days.

(TONE)

Q: Why are they going to stop working?

A. They've been working at the telescope for two days.
B. They can't find the microscope.
C. They've been working in the laboratory for two hours.
D. They can't fix the microphone.

* microscope ('maɪkrə,skop) *n.* 顯微鏡
telescope ('tɛlə,skop) *n.* 望遠鏡
laboratory ('læbrə,torɪ) *n.* 實驗室

Part D

46. (**D**) Mrs. Jones loves Mexican food. Almost every weekend she goes out to a Mexican restaurant with her husband. Now, she is taking a Mexican cooking class.

(TONE)
Q: What do Mr. and Mrs. Jones do almost every weekend?
A. Take a cooking class.
B. Have dinner at home.
C. Go to Mexico.
D. Go out to a Mexican restaurant.

* *cooking class* 烹飪課程

47. (**B**) Alex found his college years to be very busy. He enjoyed studying biology, but every weekend he drove to his parent's house to visit and during the vacations he worked in a restaurant for extra money.

(TONE)
Q: What did Alex do at college?
A. Studied biographies.
B. Kept busy.
C. Visited his parents.
D. Worked in a restaurant.

* extra（ˈɛkstrə ）adj. 額外的

48. (**D**) Jane loves cats. She has five cats at home. Her favorite is Tama. Tama is not the cutest but is the youngest of her cats. Jane likes Tama best because every morning Tama jumps on Jane's bed and wakes her up.

(TONE)
Q: Why does Jane like Tama the best?
A. Tama is the cutest cat.
B. Tama sleeps with her.
C. Tama is the youngest cat.
D. Tama wakes her up.

49. (**B**) I read the newspaper for about twenty minutes every morning after breakfast. First I look at the sports page. After that I read the comics. Then I read the front page. I read the business section last.

(TONE)
Q: Which part of the newspaper does the speaker look at first?
A. The front page.
B. The sports page.
C. The comics.
D. The business section.

* comics ('kɑmɪks) *n.* 漫畫   *front page* 頭版

50. (**B**) Paging Mr. Douglas Hanwell. If Mr. Douglas Hanwell of Lexington Shipping Corporation is on the premises, would he please come to the reception desk in the main lobby or call extension 19?

(TONE)
Q: What does Mr. Hanwell do?
A. He works for a hotel.
B. He works for a transport company.
C. He works in reception.
D. He's a telephone engineer.

* page (pedʒ) *v.* 呼名找人   premises ('prɛmɪsɪz) *n.pl.* 土地
reception desk 接待處；（旅館的）櫃台
extension (ɪk'stɛnʃən) *n.* 分機   *transport company* 運輸公司

51. (**C**) And here is WBTV's ten o'clock news bulletin. I'm Robert
Head. Towns in the southern part of the state were back on
the national grid again early this afternoon after nearly 48
hours without electricity. Hurricane Gloria downed power
lines Wednesday evening, leaving almost the entire area
without power.

    (TONE)
    Q: At what time of day was this bulletin broadcast?
    A. Morning.
    B. Afternoon.
    C. Night.
    D. It's impossible to tell.

    * bulletin ('bʊlətɪn) *n.* 新聞快報   grid (grɪd) *n.* 輸電網路
      power line 電線   down (daʊn) *v.* 打倒；擊落

52. (**C**) Good morning, ladies and gentlemen. This is your captain
speaking. It seems that cloud cover over Seattle this morning
is very low, and with visibility of only 1,100 feet we have been
advised by ground control that we will be unable to land. We
are therefore going to proceed to Portland, which will take an
extra 45 minutes. Arrival time in Portland will be 11:45.

    (TONE)
    Q: What time will the flight arrive?
    A. 11:00.
    B. A quarter to five.
    C. 11:45.
    D. At four or five.

    * captain ('kæptɪn) *n.* 機長   visibility (ˌvɪzə'bɪlətɪ) *n.* 能見度
      ground control （機場）地面管制中心
      proceed (prə'sid) *v.* 前進   flight (flaɪt) *n.* 班機

53. (**B**) We have three basic types: a checking account, a savings account, or a savings-checking account. The checking account is appropriate for people who need to make a great deal of payments by check each month. The savings account is better for people who have a lot of money to save, and would like to gain interest on it.

(TONE)

Q: Who is the checking account appropriate for?

A. People who use a credit card a lot.

B. People who make many monthly payments by check.

C. People who have a large amount of money.

D. People who need to start saving.

* ***checking account*** 活期存款帳戶　　***savings account*** 儲蓄存款帳戶
appropriate (ə'proprɪˌɪt) *adj.* 適合的　　payment ('pemənt) *n.* 付款
interest ('ɪntərɪst) *n.* 利息　　monthly ('mʌnθlɪ) *adj.* 每月的

54. (**C**) The current practice of drift net fishing will ultimately destroy fish stocks in the Pacific. Unlike a conventional net, a drift net catches anything that crosses its path.

(TONE)

Q: How does a drift net differ from a conventional net?

A. It catches only target fish.

B. It is smaller.

C. It is indiscriminate in what it catches.

D. It is used only in the Pacific Ocean.

* current ('kɜ˞ənt) *adj.* 目前的　　practice ('præktɪs) *n.* 應用
drift net 漂網　　ultimately ('ʌltəmɪtlɪ) *adv.* 最後
stocks (stɑks) *n.pl.* 資源
conventional (kən'vɛnʃənḷ) *adj.* 普通的
target ('tɑrgɪt) *n.* 目標
indiscriminate (ˌɪndɪ'skrɪmənɪt) *adj.* 不加選擇的

55. (**C**) From tomorrow through Saturday, Super Saver Hardware's mid-summer clearance sale is on. We're slashing prices on everything from power saws to lawn mowers. And to make sure you'll get there in time for all the savings, for the next seven days our doors will be open from 9:00 a.m. until 12:00 midnight.

(TONE)

Q: What are the store's hours during the sale?

A. From 9:00 a.m. to 8:00 p.m.

B. From 9:00 a.m. to 9:00 p.m.

C. From 9:00 a.m. to midnight.

D. From noon to 9:00 p.m.

* midsummer (ˈmɪdˌsʌmɚ) *n.* 盛夏；仲夏
　　clearance sale 清倉大拍賣　　slash (slæʃ) *v.* 大幅減少
　　power saw 電鋸　　*lawn mower* 割草機
　　hours (aʊrz) *n.pl.* 營業時間

56. (**B**) Farmers and government officials still haven't succeeded in reaching an agreement on the issue of opening the wheat market. Today's meeting broke up at 7:00 p.m., two hours ahead of schedule, and further meetings have been called off.

(TONE)

Q: What has been canceled?

A. Today's meeting.

B. Additional meetings.

C. Future farm subsidies.

D. Yesterday's agreement.

* issue (ˈɪʃu) *n.* 問題　　wheat (hwit) *n.* 小麥
　　break up 破裂　　further (ˈfɝðɚ) *adj.* 進一步的
　　additional (əˈdɪʃən!) *adj.* 額外的　　subsidy (ˈsʌbsədɪ) *n.* 補助金

57. (**A**) I'm sorry, Mr. Kirk, I can't give you a license. You forgot to give a right turn signal several blocks back and you went too quickly in the 25 mile an hour school zone. You'll have to take the road test again.

(TONE)
Q: Who is the person speaking?
A. An examiner.
B. A taxi driver.
C. A school teacher.
D. A banker.

* license ('laɪsn̩s) *n.* 執照　　block (blɑk) *n.* 街區
examiner (ɪg'zæmɪnɚ) *n.* 主考官

58. (**A**) In order to safeguard against acts of terrorism, we ask passengers to observe certain basic safety rules. Firstly, do not leave baggage unattended at any point within the air terminal. Secondly, do not accept any gifts or packages as carry-ons. And finally, do not allow anyone else to pack your bags for you.

(TONE)
Q: Where is this announcement being made?
A. In an airport.
B. At a port.
C. In a city office.
D. At a train station.

* safeguard ('sef,gɑrd) *v.* 保護　　terrorism ('tɛrɚ,ɪzəm) *n.* 恐怖主義
baggage ('bægɪdʒ) *n.* 行李
unattended (,ʌnə'tɛndɪd) *adj.* 無人照顧的
air terminal 航站候機室
carry-on ('kærɪ'ɑn) *n.* 隨身帶上機的行李　　pack (pæk) *v.* 打包

59. (**C**) With an Inter-Rail pass for travel in Europe you can use the freedom and flexibility of rail travel to create your own voyage of discovery. Inter-Rail allows you to enjoy a whole month's unlimited second-class travel on the national railways of 26 European and Mediterranean countries.

(TONE)

Q: What does an Inter-Rail pass allow you to enjoy?

A. A first-class train ride all the way across Europe.

B. Only three days of train travel among major European capitals.

C. A whole month's unlimited second-class train travel.

D. A two-month uninterrupted trip by train.

* **Inter-Rail pass** （歐洲）火車聯營票
flexibility（ˌflɛksəˈbɪlətɪ）n. 彈性　　voyage（ˈvɔɪdʒ）n. 旅行
Mediterranean（ˌmɛdətəˈrenɪən）adj. 地中海的
capital（ˈkæpət!）n. 首都
uninterrupted（ˌʌnɪntəˈrʌptɪd）adj. 不間斷的

60. (**A**) People who drink more than three cups of coffee a day know how awful they can feel when they can't get their caffeine. Now a study reveals that even those who sip just two or three cups a day can become anxious, sleepy and depressed if they give up coffee too quickly.

(TONE)

Q: What does the study reveal about moderate drinkers who give up coffee too fast?

A. They sometimes get anxious and depressed.

B. They usually need to see a doctor to receive medication.

C. They don't develop symptoms at first.

D. They feel worse when they return to coffee drinking.

* caffeine（ˈkæfiɪn）n. 咖啡因　　sip（sɪp）v. 小口喝
anxious（ˈæŋkʃəs）adj. 焦慮的　　medication（ˌmɛdɪˈkeʃən）n. 藥物治療
develop（dɪˈvɛləp）v. 顯現　　symptom（ˈsɪmptəm）n. 症狀

English Listening Comprehension Test

Test Book No. 13

This listening comprehension test will test your ability to understand spoken English. In this test, each conversation, statement and question will be spoken JUST ONE TIME. They will not be written out for you. There are four parts to this test. Special instructions will be given to you at the beginning of each part.

Part A

In Part A, you will see several pictures in your test book. For each picture, you will be asked 1 to 3 questions. For each question, you will hear four possible answers. Choose the best answer according to what you see in the picture.

Example:

You will see:

You will hear: What is this?
           A. This is a table.
           B. This is a chair.
           C. This is a watch.
           D. This is a doll.

The best answer to the question "What is this?" is B: "This is a chair." Therefore, you should choose answer B.

A. <u>Questions 1-4</u>

C. <u>Questions 9-11</u>

B. <u>Questions 5-8</u>

D. <u>Questions 12-15</u>

Part B

In Part B, you will hear 15 questions. After you hear a question, read the four possible answers in your test book and decide which one is the best answer to the question you have heard.

Example:

You will hear: What does your father do?

You will read: A. He's 50 years old.
B. He's a teacher.
C. He's hungry.
D. He's in Los Angeles.

The best answer to the question "What does your father do?" is B: "He's a teacher." Therefore, you should choose answer B.

Please go to the next page.

16. A. How do you do?
    B. Good morning.
    C. See you later.
    D. How are you?

17. A. That's all right.
    B. No, I am not.
    C. Yes, he does.
    D. Yes, he is.

18. A. Helen didn't do it.
    B. Helen washed yesterday.
    C. Helen did.
    D. Helen did it this morning.

19. A. How nice is it!
    B. I bought something in that store yesterday.
    C. Is that store on sale?
    D. We can go there and buy some things we need.

20. A. He just caught a cold.
    B. Something will happen to her.
    C. She was sick.
    D. She is right.

21. A. Very soon.
    B. In five minutes.
    C. Every three minutes.
    D. About five minutes.

22. A. Because I'm going to have an English test.
    B. I became interested in all the subjects.
    C. I was bored with all the subjects.
    D. Because I got good grades in English.

23. A. Mary called up.
    B. Tom calls for me.
    C. It is Peter.
    D. I called Mary up.

24. A. Fine, thanks.
    B. Yes, I did.
    C. Yes, we have.
    D. Yes, I have.

25. A. I'll take a bus.
　　B. I'll go in the morning.
　　C. I'll walk there.
　　D. I'll go to my friend's.

26. A. I bought it five hundred
　　　dollars.
　　B. My sweater took me five
　　　hundred dollars.
　　C. It costs too much.
　　D. I spent three hundred
　　　dollars on it.

27. A. Not at all.
　　B. O.K.　That is a good idea.
　　C. No, please.
　　D. Yes, thanks.

28. A. Yes, I do.
　　B. Yes, please.
　　C. Please, I do.
　　D. Yes, I do, please.

29. A. Ten minutes.
　　B. It's a long way.
　　C. It's five minutes slow.
　　D. It isn't far.

30. A. He is a soldier.
　　B. He is Mr. Green, my doctor.
　　C. He is a tall man.
　　D. He is very well.

Part C

In Part C, you will hear 15 conversations between a man and a woman. After each conversation, you will hear a question about the conversation. After you hear the question, read the four possible answers in your test book and choose the best answer to the question you have heard.

Example:

<u>You will hear:</u> (Man)   How do you go to school every day?
                      (Woman)   Usually by bus. Sometimes by taxi.

                      TONE: How does the woman go to school?

<u>You will read:</u> A. She always goes to school on foot.
                      B. She usually takes a bike.
                      C. She takes either a bus or a taxi.
                      D. She usually goes to school by bus, never by
                          taxi.

The best answer to the question "How does the woman go to school?" is C: "She takes either a bus or a taxi." Therefore, you should choose answer C.

Please go to the next page. ⇨

31. A. The cablevision is not working.
    B. All of them but channel seventeen.
    C. Channel seventeen.
    D. All of them.

32. A. Mr. Davis.
    B. Mr. Davis' secretary.
    C. Mr. Ward.
    D. Mr. Thomas.

33. A. At a bank.
    B. At a grocery store.
    C. At a doctor's office.
    D. At a gas station.

34. A. The man is too tired to go to the movie.
    B. The woman wants to go to the movie.
    C. The man wants to go out to dinner.
    D. The woman does not want to go to the movie.

35. A. He will borrow some typing paper from the woman.
    B. He will lend the woman some typing paper.
    C. He will type the woman's paper.
    D. He will buy some typing paper for the woman.

36. A. $60.
    B. $100.
    C. $120.
    D. $200.

37. A. Two blocks.
    B. Three blocks.
    C. Four blocks.
    D. Five blocks.

38. A. In a library.
    B. In a hotel.
    C. In a hospital.
    D. In an elevator.

39. A. The man's father did not go.
    B. The man thought that the game was excellent.
    C. They thought that the game was unsatisfactory.
    D. The man thought that the game was excellent, but his father thought that it was unsatisfactory.

40. A. $150.
    B. $175.
    C. $200.
    D. $225.

41. A. Patient-Doctor.
    B. Waitress-Customer.
    C. Wife-Husband.
    D. Secretary-Boss.

42. A. That the speakers did not
       go to the meeting.
    B. That the woman went to
       the meeting, but the man
       did not.
    C. That the man went to the
       meeting, but the woman
       did not.
    D. That both speakers went
       to the meeting.

43. A. By December thirtieth.
    B. By New Year's.
    C. By December third.
    D. By December thirteenth.

44. A. The operator.
    B. The person receiving the
       call.
    C. The person making the call.
    D. No one.   The call is free.

45. A. At the bank.
    B. At the market.
    C. At the nursery.
    D. At the hardware store.

Part D

In Part D, you will hear 15 short talks.   After each talk, you will hear a question about the talk.   After you hear the question, read the four possible answers in your test book and choose the best answer to the question you have heard.

Example:

You will hear: Well, that's all for Unit 15.   For today's homework, please do the review questions on page 80, and we'll check the answers tomorrow. Now, let's go on to Unit 16.

TONE: What is the teacher going to do next in today's class?

You will read: A. Check the homework.
B. Review Unit 15.
C. Start a new unit.
D. Answer students' questions.

The best answer to the question "What is the teacher going to do next in today's class?" is C: "Start a new unit."   Therefore, you should choose answer C.

Please go to the next page. ⇨

46. A. He goes swimming.
    B. He goes fishing.
    C. He takes a long walk.
    D. He works in the field.

47. A. He used a stove and burned wood.
    B. He lived on an island.
    C. He shopped on the mainland.
    D. He took a ferry.

48. A. He had been to the town before.
    B. He asked a policeman for help.
    C. His friends gave him a clear map.
    D. His map was difficult to understand.

49. A. She takes a bus.
    B. She takes a train.
    C. She takes an extra two hours.
    D. She plans to take a plane.

50. A. A computer engineer.
    B. A salesperson.
    C. A track athlete.
    D. A computer expert.

51. A. A dance.
    B. A barbecue.
    C. A cooking class.
    D. An outdoor theater production.

52. A. 10.00 seconds.
    B. 10.02 seconds.
    C. 10.22 seconds.
    D. 10.20 seconds.

53. A. Smoking at home.
    B. Smoking in all New York restaurants, regardless of size.
    C. Changing the regulations on smoking.
    D. Smoking in almost all public places in New York.

54. A. Food and oxygen.
    B. Food and water.
    C. Water and beauty.
    D. Diversity and proportion.

55. A. California's is about the
 same as Australia's.
 B. California's is about twenty
 times larger.
 C. California's is nearly two
 times larger.
 D. California's is about half
 of Australia's.

56. A. Gram.
 B. Vitamin B.
 C. Ascorbic acid.
 D. Health tip.

57. A. To make flour.
 B. To take the place of rice.
 C. To give food a different taste.
 D. To process a food.

58. A. A college professor.
 B. A book salesman.
 C. A librarian.
 D. A poet.

59. A. The whole of it.
 B. None of it.
 C. The east side.
 D. The west side.

60. A. The cafés served a wide
 variety of food.
 B. The cups of coffee were
 much larger.
 C. The customers had their
 favorite waiters.
 D. The customers could relax
 for hours over coffee.

Listening Test 13 詳解

Part A

For questions number 1 to 4, please look at picture A.

1. (**B**) Question number 1, what is the boy taking out of the refrigerator?
    A. He is getting some fruit.
    B. He is getting some cola.
    C. He is getting some cake.
    D. He is getting some groceries.

2. (**C**) Question number 2, please look at picture A again.   What is the boy on the left doing?
    A. He is drinking.
    B. He is opening a Coca-Cola.
    C. He is pouring tea.
    D. He is making tea.

    * *pour tea* 倒茶   *make tea* 泡茶

3. (**D**) Question number 3, please look at picture A again.   What is under the table?
    A. There is a thermos.   B. There is a teapot.
    C. There is a chair.   D. There is a book.

    * thermos ('θɜməs) *n.* 熱水瓶   teapot ('ti‚pɑt) *n.* 茶壺

4. (**D**) Question number 4, please look at picture A again.   What is the girl doing?
    A. She is drinking tea.
    B. She is drinking coke.
    C. She is pouring.
    D. She is pointing.

For questions number 5 to 8, please look at picture B.

5. (**B**) Question number 5, what is the girl doing?

    A. She is cutting bread.

    B. She is carrying a tray.

    C. She is pouring juice.

    D. She is making a sandwich.

    * tray〔tre〕*n.* 托盤

6. (**A**) Question number 6, please look at picture B again. What is on the tray?

    A. There is a pitcher and a piece of cake.

    B. There is bread.

    C. There are four children.

    D. There is a boy.

    * pitcher〔'pɪtʃɚ〕*n.* 水壺

7. (**C**) Question number 7, please look at picture B again. How much bread has been cut?

    A. One piece has been cut.

    B. One loaf has been cut.

    C. Two slices have been cut.

    D. Two plates have been cut.

    * loaf〔lof〕*n.* 一條（土司麵包）

    slice〔slaɪs〕*n.* 一片（麵包、火腿等）   plate〔plet〕*n.* 大的淺盤

8. (**B**) Question number 8, please look at picture B again. What is the seated boy doing?

    A. He is holding a plate.

    B. He is holding a glass.

    C. He is standing up.

    D. He is cutting bread.

    * seated〔'sitɪd〕*adj.* 坐著的

For questions number 9 to 11, please look at picture C.

9. (**B**)　Question number 9, what is the family doing?
　　　　A. They are having a party.
　　　　B. They are picnicking.
　　　　C. They are playing.
　　　　D. They are working.

10. (**C**)　Question number 10, please look at picture C again.　How
　　　　many plates are there on the table?
　　　　A. One.　　　　　　　B. Two.
　　　　C. Three.　　　　　　D. Four.

11. (**C**)　Question number 11, please look at picture C again.　Who is
　　　　at the table?
　　　　A. The man, woman, girl, and boy are at the table.
　　　　B. The girl and the boy are at the table.
　　　　C. The man, woman, and the girl are at the table.
　　　　D. The man and the woman are at the table.

For questions number 12 to 15, please look at picture D.

12. (**B**)　Question number 12, how many rooms do you see in the picture?
　　　　A. There are a bathroom and two bedrooms.
　　　　B. There are a living room, a kitchen, and a dining room.
　　　　C. There are a bedroom and a living room.
　　　　D. There are a living room, a bathroom, and a dining room.

13. (**D**)　Question number 13, please look at picture D again.　What is
　　　　the woman doing?
　　　　A. She is watching TV.
　　　　B. She is washing her face.
　　　　C. She is eating.
　　　　D. She is cooking.

14. (**A**) Question number 14, please look at picture D again. What is placed on the table next to the sofa?
   A. The table lamp.
   B. The picture.
   C. The curtain.
   D. The cupboard.

   * *table lamp* 檯燈　　curtain (ˋkɝtn) *n.* 簾子
   cupboard (ˋkʌbəd) *n.* 櫥櫃

15. (**C**) Question number 15, please look at picture D again. How many chairs are there in the dining room?
   A. There are two.
   B. There are three.
   C. There are four.
   D. There are five.

Part B

16. (**C**) So long, my friend.
   A. How do you do?　　B. Good morning.
   C. See you later.　　D. How are you?

17. (**C**) Does your father work in the office today?
   A. That's all right.　　B. No, I am not.
   C. Yes, he does.　　D. Yes, he is.

18. (**C**) Who did it yesterday?
   A. Helen didn't do it.
   B. Helen washed yesterday.
   C. Helen did.
   D. Helen did it this morning.

19. (**D**)　Everything is on sale in that store today.
    A.　How nice is it!
    B.　I bought something in that store yesterday.
    C.　Is that store on sale?
    D.　We can go there and buy some things we need.

20. (**C**)　What happened to her?
    A.　He just caught a cold.
    B.　Something will happen to her.
    C.　She was sick.
    D.　She is right.

21. (**C**)　How often does he look at the clock?
    A.　Very soon.
    B.　In five minutes.
    C.　Every three minutes.
    D.　About five minutes.

22. (**C**)　Why did you feel tired today?
    A.　Because I'm going to have an English test.
    B.　I became interested in all the subjects.
    C.　I was bored with all the subjects.
    D.　Because I got good grades in English.

23. (**C**)　Who is that on the telephone?
    A.　Mary called up.   B.　Tom calls for me.
    C.　It is Peter.   D.　I called Mary up.

24. (**B**)　Did you have a good time?
    A.　Fine, thanks.   B.　Yes, I did.
    C.　Yes, we have.   D.　Yes, I have.

25. (**D**) What will you do on Sunday?
  A. I'll take a bus.
  B. I'll go in the morning.
  C. I'll walk there.
  D. I'll go to my friend's.

26. (**D**) How much did your sweater cost?
  A. I bought it five hundred dollars.
  B. My sweater took me five hundred dollars.
  C. It costs too much.
  D. I spent three hundred dollars on it.

27. (**B**) What about going to the movies?
  A. Not at all.
  B. O.K. That is a good idea.
  C. No, please.
  D. Yes, thanks.

28. (**B**) Would you like a cup of tea?
  A. Yes, I do.   B. Yes, please.
  C. Please, I do. D. Yes, I do, please.

29. (**A**) How long does it take?
  A. Ten minutes.
  B. It's a long way.
  C. It's five minutes slow.
  D. It isn't far.

30. (**B**) Who is that man?
  A. He is a soldier.
  B. He is Mr. Green, my doctor.
  C. He is a tall man.
  D. He is very well.

Part C

31. (**C**)　W: There's something wrong with the TV.　Only channel
　　　　　　 seventeen has a good picture.
　　　　　M: Maybe the cablevision isn't working.

　　　　　(TONE)
　　　　　Q: Which channel has a good picture?
　　　　　A. The cablevision is not working.
　　　　　B. All of them but channel seventeen.
　　　　　C. Channel seventeen.
　　　　　D. All of them.
　　　　　* cablevision ('kebḷˏvɪʒən) *n.* 有線電視 (= *cable television*)

32. (**C**)　M: Hello.　I'd like to speak with Mr. Davis, please.　This is
　　　　　　 Thomas Ward with the Office of Immigrations.
　　　　　W: I'm sorry, Mr. Ward.　Mr. Davis is in conference now.

　　　　　(TONE)
　　　　　Q: Who works for the Immigrations Office?
　　　　　A. Mr. Davis.
　　　　　B. Mr. Davis' secretary.
　　　　　C. Mr. Ward.
　　　　　D. Mr. Thomas.
　　　　　* *the Office of Immigrations* 移民局；入出境管理局
　　　　　 in conference 開會中

33. (**D**)　W: Fill it up with regular and check the oil, please.
　　　　　M: Right away, Miss.

(TONE)

Q: Where did this conversation most probably take place?

A. At a bank.

B. At a grocery store.

C. At a doctor's office.

D. At a gas station.

* ***fill up*** 加滿　　regular (ˈrɛgjələ) *adj.* (汽油) 普通的；一般的
oil (ɔɪl) *n.* 機油

34. (**D**) M: Let's go to the movies after dinner.

W: Well, I'll go if you really want to, but I'm a little bit tired.

(TONE)

Q: What conclusion does the woman want us to make from her statement?

A. The man is too tired to go to the movie.

B. The woman wants to go to the movie.

C. The man wants to go out to dinner.

D. The woman does not want to go to the movie.

35. (**D**) W: I'm out of typing paper.　Will you lend me some?

M: I don't have any either, but I'll be glad to get you some when I go to the bookstore.

(TONE)

Q: What is the man going to do?

A. He will borrow some typing paper from the woman.

B. He will lend the woman some typing paper.

C. He will type the woman's paper.

D. He will buy some typing paper for the woman.

* ***be out of*** 用完~

36. (**A**) W: I like these chairs. How much are they?

M: They are sixty dollars each or one hundred dollars for the pair.

(TONE)

Q: How much does one chair cost?

A. $60.   B. $100.
C. $120.   D. $200.

37. (**D**) M: Excuse me. Could you please tell me how to get to the University City Bank?

W: Sure. Go straight for two blocks, then turn left and walk three more blocks until you get to the drugstore. It's right across the street.

(TONE)

Q: How far must the man walk to get to the bank?

A. Two blocks.   B. Three blocks.
C. Four blocks.   D. Five blocks.

38. (**C**) M: Excuse me, nurse. I'm looking for the emergency room. I thought that it was on the first floor.

W: It is. This is the basement. Take the elevator one flight up and turn left.

(TONE)

Q: Where did this conversation most probably take place?

A. In a library.

B. In a hotel.

C. In a hospital.

D. In an elevator.

* *emergency room* 急診室   basement ('besmənt) *n.* 地下室

39. (**C**) W: How did you and your dad like the football game yesterday?
M: Oh. They played so poorly that we left at half-time.

(TONE)
Q: How did the man and his father feel about the football game?
A. The man's father did not go.
B. The man thought that the game was excellent.
C. They thought that the game was unsatisfactory.
D. The man thought that the game was excellent, but his father thought that it was unsatisfactory.

40. (**B**) M: How much is the rent?
W: It's a hundred and fifty dollars a month unfurnished or two hundred dollars a month furnished. Utilities are twenty-five dollars extra.

(TONE)
Q: How much will it cost the man to rent an unfurnished apartment, including utilities?
A. $150.   B. $175.
C. $200.   D. $225.

* rent (rɛnt) *n.* 租金   unfurnished (ʌn'fɜnɪʃt) *adj.* 沒有家具的
furnished ('fɜnɪʃt) *adj.* 有家具的
utility (ju'tɪlətɪ) *n.* 用具（實用性）

41. (**B**) W: Would you like to see a menu?
M: No, thank you. I already know what I want to order.

(TONE)
Q: What is the probable relationship between the two speakers?
A. Patient-Doctor.
B. Waitress-Customer.
C. Wife-Husband.
D. Secretary-Boss.

42. (**A**) W: Didn't you go to the meeting last night either?
　　　　　M: No.　I had a slight headache.

　　　　　(TONE)
　　　　　Q: What do we understand from this conversation?
　　　　　A. That the speakers did not go to the meeting.
　　　　　B. That the woman went to the meeting, but the man did not.
　　　　　C. That the man went to the meeting, but the woman did not.
　　　　　D. That both speakers went to the meeting.

43. (**D**) W: Your library books are due on December thirteenth.　If
　　　　　　you haven't finished using them by then, you may renew
　　　　　　them once.
　　　　　M: Thank you very much.　I only need them for a few days.

　　　　　(TONE)
　　　　　Q: When must the man return his books to the library?
　　　　　A. By December thirtieth.　　B. By New Year's.
　　　　　C. By December third.　　　　D. By December thirteenth.

　　　　* renew (rɪˋnju) *v.* 更新

44. (**B**) M: Operator, I want to place a long distance call collect to
　　　　　　Columbus, Ohio.　The area code is six-one-four and the
　　　　　　number is four-two-nine, seven-five-eight-three.
　　　　　W: Thank you.　I'll ring it for you.

　　　　　(TONE)
　　　　　Q: Who will pay for the call?
　　　　　A. The operator.
　　　　　B. The person receiving the call.
　　　　　C. The person making the call.
　　　　　D. No one.　The call is free.

　　　　* collect (kəˋlɛkt) *adv.* 對方付費　　*area code* 區域號碼
　　　　ring (rɪŋ) *v.* 打電話

45. (**B**) M: Can you lend me ten dollars until tomorrow?

W: I just spent my last dollar for groceries. I wish you had asked me an hour ago.

(TONE)

Q: Where has the woman just been?

A. At the bank.

B. At the market.

C. At the nursery.

D. At the hardware store.

* nursery ('nʒsərɪ) *n.* 托兒所   ***hardware store*** 五金行

Part D

46. (**C**) Lisa's grandfather is an early riser. He lives in the country near the sea. He gets up at 4:00 every morning and walks for an hour before breakfast. After breakfast he works in the field or goes fishing.

(TONE)

Q: What does Lisa's grandfather do before breakfast?

A. He goes swimming.

B. He goes fishing.

C. He takes a long walk.

D. He works in the field.

47. (**A**) Mike's uncle once lived on an island where there were few other people. He had to cut wood to heat his stove because there was no gas or electricity. To do his shopping, he had to take a ferry boat to the mainland.

(TONE)

Q: What did Mike's uncle do for heat?

A. He used a stove and burned wood.

B. He lived on an island.

C. He shopped on the mainland.

D. He took a ferry.

* heat (hit) *v.* 加熱　　*ferry boat* 渡船
mainland ('men,lænd) *n.* 大陸

48. (**D**) Paul usually arrives early, but yesterday he didn't.　He was trying to meet his friends in a town he didn't know very well, and he got lost.　This was because his map was so unclear that he couldn't understand it.　Eventually, Paul asked a policeman for help, and he found his friends.

(TONE)

Q: Why did Paul get lost?

A. He had been to the town before.

B. He asked a policeman for help.

C. His friends gave him a clear map.

D. His map was difficult to understand.

49. (**B**) Sally went to New York City last week.　Although she usually rides a train into the city, last week she went there by car.　That was a mistake.　The roads were so crowded that it took her an extra two hours.　Next time, she plans to take the train again.

(TONE)

Q: How does Sally usually go to New York?

A. She takes a bus.

B. She takes a train.

C. She takes an extra two hours.

D. She plans to take a plane.

50. (**B**)　HGC Computers has an opening in its sales division starting
May 1st.　Applicants should have a proven track record in
sales.　Previous experience need not necessarily be in the
computer industry, but a basic knowledge of computers is
essential.　Preference will be given to applicants in their 30s,
but motivated achievers in their 20s with experience in
computers sales are also welcome to apply.

(TONE)
Q: What is this company looking for?
A. A computer engineer.
B. A salesperson.
C. A track athlete.
D. A computer expert.

* division (də'vɪʒən) *n.* 部門　　applicant ('æpləkənt) *n.* 申請人
 track record 銷售記錄　　preference ('prɛfərəns) *n.* 優先權
 motivated ('motə,vetɪd) *adj.* 有動機的　　track (træk) *n.* 徑賽

51. (**B**)　The Cape Worth District Youth Club is sponsoring a cookout
in the clubhouse grounds on Saturday, September 21st,
starting at 12:30.　The entrance fee is $5, and this includes
food and soft drinks.

(TONE)
Q: What kind of event is taking place on September 21st?
A. A dance.
B. A barbecue.
C. A cooking class.
D. An outdoor theater production.

* district ('dɪstrɪkt) *n.* 地區　　sponsor ('spɑnsə) *v.* 贊助；主辦
 cookout ('kʊk,aʊt) *n.* 野外烹飪　　***entrance fee*** 入場費
 barbecue ('bɑrbɪ,kju) *n.* 烤肉

52. (.**B**) Well, that certainly was one of the best 100-meter finals
we've seen this season. Brandon Christopher managed to
edge ahead in the last 10 meters, giving him a winning time
of 10.02 seconds, just 1/100 of a second ahead of Larry Bartell.

(TONE)
Q: What was the winning time for the race?
A. 10.00 seconds.   B. 10.02 seconds.
C. 10.22 seconds.   D. 10.20 seconds.

* final (ˈfaɪnl̩) *n.* 決賽   *edge ahead* 慢慢移動

53. (**D**) How would you like to live in a place where you can't smoke in
restaurants, outdoor stadiums, zoos or offices? Not much
fun if you're a smoker, right? Well, that's exactly what
happened in New York City recently. The mayor banned
smoking in almost all public places, claiming that thousands
and thousands of lives have been destroyed by smoking.

(TONE)
Q: What does the new law prohibit?
A. Smoking at home.
B. Smoking in all New York restaurants, regardless of size.
C. Changing the regulations on smoking.
D. Smoking in almost all public places in New York.

* stadium (ˈstedɪəm) *n.* 體育場   ban (bæn) *v.* 禁止
   claim (klem) *v.* 宣稱   prohibit (prəˈnɪbɪt) *v.* 禁止

54. (**A**) Plants are vital to our existence. For one thing, they give us
oxygen. Secondly, they give us food—we eat their seeds,
their leaves, and their fruit. But plants do much, much more
than just give us life—they give us beauty. Who can deny
the natural beauty of flowers and shrubs, with their infinite
number of colors, fragrances, and shapes?

(TONE)

Q: What do plants give people?

A. Food and oxygen.

B. Food and water.

C. Water and beauty.

D. Diversity and proportion.

* *for one thing* 一方面　　shrub〔ʃrʌb〕*n.* 灌木
infinite〔'ɪnfənɪt〕*adj.* 無限的　　fragrance〔'fregrəns〕*n.* 芳香
diversity〔daɪ'vɝsətɪ〕*n.* 多樣性
proportion〔prə'pɔrʃən〕*n.* 比例；均衡

55. (**C**) Australia is larger and smaller than California.　It depends on what you compare.　In population, California is the larger of the two.　The state of California has almost twice as many people as the country of Australia.　But in size, Australia is far larger, of course, with an area almost twenty times California's.

(TONE)

Q: How can we compare the populations of Australia and California?

A. California's is about the same as Australia's.

B. California's is about twenty times larger.

C. California's is nearly two times larger.

D. California's is about half of Australia's.

56. (**C**) I'm Maria Morgan with today's health tip.　It's very important that you get plenty of ascorbic acid—in other words, vitamin C. A good source of vitamin C is citrus fruit; for example, oranges, grapefruits, and lemons.　Although most people know this already, many don't know that some vegetables, such as broccoli, potatoes, and cabbage, are also rich in vitamin C.

(TONE)

Q: What term does the speaker define?

A. Gram.

B. Vitamin B.

C. Ascorbic acid.

D. Health tip.

* tip〔tɪp〕*n.* 小祕方　　ascorbic〔əˈskɔrbɪk〕*adj.* 抗壞血病的
acid〔ˈæsɪd〕*n.* 酸　　***ascorbic acid*** 抗壞血酸；維他命 C
citrus〔ˈsɪtrəs〕*adj.* 柑橘屬的　　broccoli〔ˈbrɑkəlɪ〕*n.* 綠花椰果
cabbage〔ˈkæbɪdʒ〕*n.* 甘藍菜；包心菜　　define〔dɪˈfaɪn〕*v.* 下定義

57. (**C**) Saffron is the most expensive spice in the world.　It's very
popular in Spain and Iran, where it is used to give, for
example rice a distinct subtle flavor.　The reason saffron is
so expensive is because of the labor involved in producing it.

(TONE)

Q: What is saffron used for?

A. To make flour.

B. To take the place of rice.

C. To give food a different taste.

D. To process a food.

* saffron〔ˈsæfrən〕*n.* 番紅花　　spice〔spaɪs〕*n.* 香料
distinct〔dɪˈstɪŋkt〕*adj.* 不同的　　subtle〔ˈsʌtḷ〕*adj.* 微妙的
flavor〔ˈflevɚ〕*n.* 味道　　labor〔ˈlebɚ〕*n.* 勞力
process〔ˈprɑsɛs〕*v.* 加工

58. (**A**) Today I'm going to talk about an American writer.　Though
he is not as well-known in American literature as such giants
as Mark Twain, Ernest Hemingway, and William Faulkner, he
nevertheless wrote some unforgettable novels and excellent
short stories.　His name is Jack London.

(TONE)

Q: Who is most probably giving this talk?

A. A college professor.

B. A book salesman.

C. A librarian.

D. A poet.

* nevertheless (ˌnɛvəðə'lɛs) adv. 然而

59. (**C**) Despite its relatively small size, the island of Hawaii has a surprisingly varied climate. The east side of the island is wet, while in contrast the west is much drier. Although the temperature stays warm all year round in most areas, the highlands around Waimea tend to be comfortably cool.

(TONE)

Q: Which part of the island gets a lot of rain?

A. The whole of it.

B. None of it.

C. The east side.

D. The west side.

* relatively ('rɛlətɪvlɪ) adv. 相對地　　varied ('vɛrɪd) adj. 變化的
all year round 一年到頭　　highland ('haɪlənd) n. 高地
tend to 傾向於

60. (**D**) Spending an hour or two sitting relaxed in a café over a cup of coffee used to be an integral part of life in France. Just for the price of a single cup of coffee, you could stay at your favorite café as long as you liked. No waiter would dream of suggesting that customers should leave before they were ready to go.

(TONE)

Q: According to the speaker, what was the best thing about cafés?

A. The cafés served a wide variety of food.

B. The cups of coffee were much larger.

C. The customers had their favorite waiters.

D. The customers could relax for hours over coffee.

* integral（ˈɪntəgrəl）*adj.* 必要的　　serve（sɜv）*v.* 供應
variety（vəˈraɪətɪ）*n.* 多樣

English Listening Comprehension Test

Test Book No. 14

This listening comprehension test will test your ability to understand spoken English. In this test, each conversation, statement and question will be spoken JUST ONE TIME. They will not be written out for you. There are four parts to this test. Special instructions will be given to you at the beginning of each part.

Part A

In Part A, you will see several pictures in your test book. For each picture, you will be asked 1 to 3 questions. For each question, you will hear four possible answers. Choose the best answer according to what you see in the picture.

Example:

You will see:

You will hear: What is this?
A. This is a table.
B. This is a chair.
C. This is a watch.
D. This is a doll.

The best answer to the question "What is this?" is B: "This is a chair." Therefore, you should choose answer B.

A. Questions 1-2

D. Questions 7-9

B. Questions 3-4

E. Questions 10-12

C. Questions 5-6

F. Questions 13-15

Part B

In Part B, you will hear 15 questions.   After you hear a question, read the four possible answers in your test book and decide which one is the best answer to the question you have heard.

Example:

You will hear: What does your father do?

You will read: A. He's 50 years old.
                  B. He's a teacher.
                  C. He's hungry.
                  D. He's in Los Angeles.

The best answer to the question "What does your father do?" is B: "He's a teacher."   Therefore, you should choose answer B.

Please go to the next page. ⟹

16. A. It's Saturday.
    B. It's cold.
    C. It's winter.
    D. It's ten o'clock.

17. A. Yes, please.
    B. Yes, but not much.
    C. Yes, many.
    D. Yes, we have a lot of.

18. A. Usually five days a week.
    B. She works only at night.
    C. She always works hard.
    D. Her work is quite easy.

19. A. He'll study English.
    B. Let's go to a movie.
    C. No, you are not going to do it.
    D. We played basketball.

20. A. That's a good idea.
    B. So do I.
    C. What's the problem?
    D. I hope so.

21. A. Good! But I have no time.
    B. Why not?
    C. What time is your flight?
    D. That's great.

22. A. She doesn't know it.
    B. Mine does, too.
    C. She must be home.
    D. Oh, doesn't she?

23. A. I'll do that, Mother.
    B. No, I don't.
    C. You are very kind to do so.
    D. No, thank you.

24. A. No, not today. Thank you.
    B. Thank you, sir.
    C. May I give you a hand?
    D. What do you need?

25. A. Excuse me. I want some.
    B. Not at all.
    C. Yes, please.
    D. Yes, I am.

26. A. The first scene has already
     started.
   B. No, I think it is your
     move, actually.
   C. I just started reading the
     book.
   D. I'm pleased to meet you.

27. A. Fine.   Let's play ball.
   B. It certainly is.
   C. I need more time to
     decide.
   D. No, not yet.

28. A. Yes, it's not.
   B. No, I am not.
   C. Yes, they are.
   D. Yes, it is.

29. A. What is it about?
   B. Not at all.   Thanks.
   C. Yes, we will.
   D. I'd love to.

30. A. I think those are my pens.
   B. I think it is my pen.
   C. I think that is my friend.
   D. I think those are my friends.

Part C

In Part C, you will hear 15 conversations between a man and a woman. After each conversation, you will hear a question about the conversation. After you hear the question, read the four possible answers in your test book and choose the best answer to the question you have heard.

Example:

<u>You will hear</u>: (Man)   How do you go to school every day?
                   (Woman) Usually by bus. Sometimes by taxi.

                   TONE: How does the woman go to school?

<u>You will read</u>: A. She always goes to school on foot.
                  B. She usually takes a bike.
                  C. She takes either a bus or a taxi.
                  D. She usually goes to school by bus, never by taxi.

The best answer to the question "How does the woman go to school?" is C: "She takes either a bus or a taxi." Therefore, you should choose answer C.

Please go to the next page. ⇨

31. A. After five.
    B. At or before five.
    C. In the morning.
    D. Late at night.

32. A. Studying.
    B. Relaxing.
    C. Taking a test.
    D. Studying subjects other
       than math.

33. A. A few days.
    B. We don't know.
    C. A couple of weeks.
    D. Just one week.

34. A. It doesn't work.
    B. It only works temporarily.
    C. It's really effective.
    D. It has harmful side effects.

35. A. She hates it.
    B. It makes her mad.
    C. She is embarrassed.
    D. She likes it very much.

36. A. He isn't interested.
    B. He's scared.
    C. He doesn't understand it.
    D. He's mad at it.

37. A. She really likes the course.
    B. She wishes she hadn't
       taken it.
    C. She thinks the course is
       too late.
    D. She has no interest in it.

38. A. He can talk without
       preparing.
    B. He can speak standing up.
    C. He likes to talk without
       thinking.
    D. He talks with his toes.

39. A. He's too embarrassed.
    B. He has no interest in that
       movie.
    C. He's boo busy.
    D. He has no money.

40. A. A credit card.
    B. A driver's license.
    C. A magazine subscription.
    D. None of the above.

41. A. California.
    B. New York.
    C. The South.
    D. Michigan.

42. A. He's angry because he lost some clothing.
    B. He's angry because he lost his money.
    C. He's sad because he lost his job.
    D. He was scolded for not wearing a shirt.

43. A. Move.
    B. Get a puppy.
    C. Transfer.
    D. Buy a cat.

44. A. A car almost hit her.
    B. She shook someone.
    C. Someone shook her.
    D. Someone chased her.

45. A. Driving in a car.
    B. Watching a movie.
    C. Eating dinner.
    D. Dancing.

Part D

In Part D, you will hear 15 short talks. After each talk, you will hear a question about the talk. After you hear the question, read the four possible answers in your test book and choose the best answer to the question you have heard.

Example:

You will hear: Well, that's all for Unit 15. For today's homework, please do the review questions on page 80, and we'll check the answers tomorrow. Now, let's go on to Unit 16.

TONE: What is the teacher going to do next in today's class?

You will read: A. Check the homework.
B. Review Unit 15.
C. Start a new unit.
D. Answer students' questions.

The best answer to the question "What is the teacher going to do next in today's class?" is C: "Start a new unit." Therefore, you should choose answer C.

Please go to the next page. ⇨

46. A. To make many friends.
    B. To have a big family.
    C. So that everyone can sit together.
    D. So that everyone can eat dinner quickly.

47. A. So that there would be no misunderstanding.
    B. So that he could buy from a local store.
    C. So that he could speak with a clerk.
    D. So that the computer software could not be found.

48. A. They like watching movies twice.
    B. They missed the beginning of the movie.
    C. They didn't find the theater after all.
    D. They didn't like that movie very much.

49. A. For her long vacation.
    B. At 10:30 in the next morning.
    C. For a couple of hours.
    D. For about seven hours.

50. A. 6.
    B. 10.
    C. 13.
    D. 30.

51. A. At an airport.
    B. At a hospital.
    C. In a department store.
    D. At a school.

52. A. 40 %.
    B. 14 %.
    C. 20 %.
    D. 26 %.

53. A. Mountain climbing.
    B. Skiing.
    C. Car racing.
    D. Windsurfing.

54. A. In Long Beach.
    B. In Sandy Head.
    C. In Cape Hook.
    D. In Silver Cup.

55. A. One of the major highways
     was shut down.
   B. There have been many
     traffic accidents.
   C. A lot of the roads are being
     repaired.
   D. Due to rain, many roads
     are flooded.

56. A. He has been given an award.
   B. He is presenting an award.
   C. He is trying to raise money.
   D. He is trying to get support.

57. A. Several million years.
   B. 10 million years.
   C. 40 million years.
   D. Over 40 million years.

58. A. In the Far North.
   B. In Oakland.
   C. In San Francisco.
   D. In New York.

59. A. The weather equipment was
     destroyed by the storms.
   B. Heavy rain damaged the
     weather equipment.
   C. The weather equipment
     was not able to pick up
     developing tornadoes.
   D. Nobody could operate the
     new weather equipment
     properly.

60. A. Half the risk for
     nonsmokers.
   B. Double the risk for
     nonsmokers.
   C. Five and a half times the
     risk for nonsmokers.
   D. 85 percent of the risk for
     nonsmokers.

Listening Test 14 詳解

Part A

For questions number 1 to 2, please look at picture A.

1. (**C**) Question number 1, what is the woman doing?
  A. She is buying a mirror.
  B. She is powdering her face.
  C. She is applying lipstick.
  D. She is searching for her contact lenses.

   * powder (ˈpaʊdɚ) v. 撲粉 apply (əˈplaɪ) v. 塗
   lipstick (ˈlɪpˌstɪk) n. 口紅

2. (**D**) Question number 2, please look at picture A again. What is she probably going to do next?
  A. She is going to take a bath.
  B. She is going to take a nap.
  C. She is going to have an operation.
  D. She is going to visit a friend.

   * *take a nap* 小睡

For questions number 3 to 4, please look at picture B.

3. (**B**) Question number 3, which holiday is it?
  A. It is Christmas.   B. It is Halloween.
  C. It is Valentine's Day. D. It is Thanksgiving.

4. (**C**) Question number 4, please look at picture B again. What are the children doing?
  A. They are painting a pumpkin.
  B. They are dressing a pumpkin.
  C. They are carving a pumpkin.
  D. They are eating a pumpkin.

   * carve (kɑrv) v. 刻 pumpkin (ˈpʌmpkɪn) n. 南瓜

For questions number 5 to 6, please look at picture C.

5. (**C**)　Question number 5, what are the customers eating?
   A. They are eating salad.
   B. They are eating bread.
   C. They are eating dessert.
   D. They are eating steak.

6. (**B**)　Question number 6, please look at picture C again.　What is the little girl eating?
   A. She is eating fruit.
   B. She is eating a sundae.
   C. She is eating a banana split.
   D. She is eating cake.

   * sundae ('sʌnde) *n.* 聖代　　***banana split*** 香蕉船

For questions number 7 to 9, please look at picture D.

7. (**C**)　Question number 7, what is this a picture of?
   A. It is a kitchen.
   B. It is a lounge.
   C. It is a laundromat.
   D. It is a warehouse.

   * lounge (laʊndʒ) *n.* 休息室　　laundromat ('lɔndrəmæt) *n.* 自助洗衣店
   warehouse ('wɛr,haʊs) *n.* 倉庫

8. (**A**)　Question number 8, please look at picture D again.　What is the woman on the right doing?
   A. She is folding clothes.
   B. She is ironing clothes.
   C. She is washing clothes.
   D. She is buying clothes.

   * fold (fold) *v.* 摺疊

9. (**C**) Question number 9, please look at picture D again. Where is the old man putting his money?

    A. He is putting money into a washing machine.

    B. He is putting money into a spinner.

    C. He is putting money into a dryer.

    D. He is putting money into a presser.

    * spinner (ˈspɪnɚ) *n.* 紡織機   dryer (ˈdraɪɚ) *n.* 乾衣機

    presser (ˈprɛsɚ) *n.* 壓榨機

For questions number 10 to 12, please look at picture E.

10. (**D**) Question number 10, how many different musical instruments are there?

    A. There are five.

    B. There are four.

    C. There are nine.

    D. There are twelve.

11. (**C**) Question number 11, please look at picture E again. What is the woman in the long dress playing?

    A. She is playing the violin.

    B. She is playing the trumpet.

    C. She is playing the flute.

    D. She is playing the cello.

    * violin (ˌvaɪəˈlɪn) *n.* 小提琴   trumpet (ˈtrʌmpɪt) *n.* 喇叭

    flute (flut) *n.* 長笛   cello (ˈtʃɛlo) *n.* 大提琴

12. (**B**) Question number 12, please look at picture E again. What is the man with beard playing?

    A. He is playing the cello.

    B. He is playing the drums.

    C. He is playing the piano.

    D. He is playing the harmonica.

    * harmonica (hɑrˈmɑnɪkə) *n.* 口琴

For questions number 13 to 15, please look at picture F.

13. (**B**) Question number 13, what is the man doing?
    A. He is walking his dog.
    B. He is mowing the grass.
    C. He is washing the clothes.
    D. He is trimming the trees.
    * mow〔mo〕v. 割　　trim〔trɪm〕v. 修剪

14. (**A**) Question number 14, please look at picture F again.　What is the woman doing?
    A. She is hanging out clothes.
    B. She is washing clothes.
    C. She is sewing clothes.
    D. She is folding clothes.
    * *hang out* 掛出

15. (**D**) Question number 15, please look at picture F again.　What are the children doing?
    A. They are answering a question.
    B. They are fighting.
    C. They are frowning.
    D. They are waving their hands.
    * frown〔fraʊn〕v. 皺眉

Part B

16. (**C**) What season is it now?
    A. It's Saturday.
    B. It's cold.
    C. It's winter.
    D. It's ten o'clock.

17. (**B**) Do we have any fruit?
        A. Yes, please.
        B. Yes, but not much.
        C. Yes, many.
        D. Yes, we have a lot of.

18. (**A**) How many days a week does Alice Jones work?
        A. Usually five days a week.
        B. She works only at night.
        C. She always works hard.
        D. Her work is quite easy.

19. (**B**) What are we going to do?
        A. He'll study English.
        B. Let's go to a movie.
        C. No, you are not going to do it.
        D. We played basketball.

20. (**C**) I can't make these nails stay in one place.
        A. That's a good idea.
        B. So do I.
        C. What's the problem?
        D. I hope so.

        * nail〔nel〕*n.* 釘子

21. (**D**) I'll drive you to the airport tomorrow.
        A. Good! But I have no time.
        B. Why not?
        C. What time is your flight?
        D. That's great.

22. (**D**) My mother never reads the newspaper.
    A. She doesn't know it.
    B. Mine does, too.
    C. She must be home.
    D. Oh, doesn't she?

23. (**A**) Take off your dirty clothes right there, Tom.
    A. I'll do that, Mother.
    B. No, I don't.
    C. You are very kind to do so.
    D. No, thank you.

24. (**A**) Would you like to buy some other things?
    A. No, not today. Thank you.
    B. Thank you, sir.
    C. May I give you a hand?
    D. What do you need?

25. (**C**) Would you like some tea?
    A. Excuse me. I want some.
    B. Not at all.
    C. Yes, please.
    D. Yes, I am.

26. (**A**) When will the movie begin?
    A. The first scene has already started.
    B. No, I think it is your move, actually.
    C. I just started reading the book.
    D. I'm pleased to meet you.
    * move〔muv〕*n.* 一步（棋）

27. (**D**)　You haven't done your homework, have you?
　　　　A. Fine.　Let's play ball.
　　　　B. It certainly is.
　　　　C. I need more time to decide.
　　　　D. No, not yet.

28. (**C**)　Are these your pictures?
　　　　A. Yes, it's not.
　　　　B. No, I am not.
　　　　C. Yes, they are.
　　　　D. Yes, it is.

29. (**C**)　Will you and John play basketball tonight?
　　　　A. What is it about?
　　　　B. Not at all.　Thanks.
　　　　C. Yes, we will.
　　　　D. I'd love to.

30. (**B**)　What is that?
　　　　A. I think those are my pens.
　　　　B. I think it is my pen.
　　　　C. I think that is my friend.
　　　　D. I think those are my friends.

Part C

31. (**B**)　W: There's no use going to the store now.
　　　　M: Yeah, you're right.　It's after five already.

　　　　(TONE)
　　　　Q: When does the store probably close?
　　　　A. After five.　　　　B. At or before five.
　　　　C. In the morning.　　D. Late at night.

32. (**A**)　M: I've been brushing up on mathematics the past few days.
　　　　　　W: Yeah, I hear that math is one of the harder sections on
　　　　　　　　the test.

　　　　　(TONE)
　　　　　Q: What has the man been doing?
　　　　　A. Studying.
　　　　　B. Relaxing.
　　　　　C. Taking a test.
　　　　　D. Studying subjects other than math.

　　　　　* ***brush up on*** 溫習～（科目）　　　section ('sɛkʃən) *n.* 部分
　　　　　other than 除了

33. (**A**)　M: Have you heard I'm going to Spain for a few days?
　　　　　　W: No.　That sounds like fun.

　　　　　(TONE)
　　　　　Q: How long will the man be gone?
　　　　　A. A few days.
　　　　　B. We don't know.
　　　　　C. A couple of weeks.
　　　　　D. Just one week.

34. (**D**)　M: Is it true you can't take this medicine?
　　　　　　W: Yes.　It works well, but the side effects are really strong.

　　　　　(TONE)
　　　　　Q: Why can't the woman take the medicine?
　　　　　A. It doesn't work.
　　　　　B. It only works temporarily.
　　　　　C. It's really effective.
　　　　　D. It has harmful side effects.

　　　　　* ***side effect*** 副作用

35. (**D**) W: I really envy Susie's tan.
    M: Give yourself time. You'll get it.

    (TONE)
    Q: How does the woman feel about Susie's tan?
    A. She hates it.
    B. It makes her mad.
    C. She is embarrassed.
    D. She likes it very much.

    * envy (ˈɛnvɪ) v. 羨慕   tan (tæn) n. 曬成的棕褐膚色

36. (**C**) M: This whole situation is a real puzzle.
    W: What are we going to do about it?

    (TONE)
    Q: How does the man feel about the situation?
    A. He isn't interested.
    B. He's scared.
    C. He doesn't understand it.
    D. He's mad at it.

    * puzzle (ˈpʌzl̩) n. 謎

37. (**B**) W: I really regret taking this course.
    M: Is it too late to drop out?

    (TONE)
    Q: What does the woman say about the course she's taking?
    A. She really likes the course.
    B. She wishes she hadn't taken it.
    C. She thinks the course is too late.
    D. She has no interest in it.

    * *drop out* 退出

38. (**A**) W: Don't you think you ought to practice your speech a little
   before you go?
   M: No, I'm not worried. I can think on my feet.

(TONE)
Q: Why is the man not worried?
A. He can talk without preparing.
B. He can speak standing up.
C. He likes to talk without thinking.
D. He talks with his toes.

* ***think on one's feet*** 反應快

39. (**D**) W: Would you like to go to the movie with us?
   M: I can't. I haven't got a red cent.

(TONE)
Q: Why can't the man go to the movies?
A. He's too embarrassed.
B. He has no interest in that movie.
C. He's too busy.
D. He has no money.

* ***red cent*** 一分錢 (= *cent*)

40. (**C**) W: I'd like to renew my subscription. It expires next month.
   M: Okay. Do you want a 1- or 2-year subscription? You get
   two extra issues with the 2-year one.

(TONE)
Q: What are the people most likely talking about?
A. A credit card.   B. A driver's license.
C. A magazine subscription.   D. None of the above.

* subscription (səb'skrɪpʃən) *n.* 訂閱   expire (ɪk'spaɪr) *v.* 到期
   issue ('ɪʃju) *n.* (刊物) 一期

41. (**B**) W: Where are you from?
        M: I was born in California, but I grew up in New York and studied in Michigan.

        (TONE)
        Q: Where did the man grow up?
        A. California.
        B. New York.
        C. The South.
        D. Michigan.

42. (**A**) W: What's up with Matt today?
        M: He lost his favorite shirt and he's really ticked off about it.

        (TONE)
        Q: What's the matter with Matt?
        A. He's angry because he lost some clothing.
        B. He's angry because he lost his money.
        C. He's sad because he lost his job.
        D. He was scolded for not wearing a shirt.
        * *tick off* 使~生氣

43. (**A**) W: My dog just had puppies. Would you like one?
        M: I can't. My wife and I are moving.

        (TONE)
        Q: What will the man do?
        A. Move.
        B. Get a puppy.
        C. Transfer.
        D. Buy a cat.
        * puppy ('pʌpɪ) *n.* 小狗

44. (**A**) W: Why is Mary so strange today?

　　　M: Someone almost ran her down when she was crossing the street, and she's still a little shaken up.

　　(TONE)
　　Q: What happened to Mary?
　　A. A car almost hit her.
　　B. She shook someone.
　　C. Someone shook her.
　　D. Someone chased her.
　　* *shake up* 使震驚

45. (**D**) W: Please, Jack.　Don't keep stepping on my feet.

　　　M: Well, if you'd keep them away from mine, you'd be all right.

　　(TONE)
　　Q: What is this couple probably doing?
　　A. Driving in a car.　　　B. Watching a movie.
　　C. Eating dinner.　　　　D. Dancing.

Part D

46. (**C**) The Coopers have a new table in their dining room.　The table is very big, so twelve people can sit together.　The Coopers have a big family and many friends.　They are happy because now everyone can sit at the same table whenever they have a family dinner.

　　(TONE)
　　Q: What did the Coopers buy a new table for?
　　A. To make many friends.
　　B. To have a big family.
　　C. So that everyone can sit together.
　　D. So that everyone can eat dinner quickly.

47. (**A**) Paul could not find the computer software he wanted in local stores, so he decided to purchase it by mail order. To avoid any misunderstanding, he decided to send the order by fax rather than speak to a clerk on the phone.

(TONE)

Q: What did Paul send his order by fax for?

A. So that there would be no misunderstanding.

B. So that he could buy from a local store.

C. So that he could speak with a clerk.

D. So that the computer software could not be found.

* software ('soft,wɛr) *n.* 軟體　　local ('lokḷ) *adj.* 當地的

48. (**B**) Last night Matt and Andrea went to the movies. They lost their way and arrived late, so they missed the first fifteen minutes of the movie. They both liked the movie so much that they decided to go again to see it from the beginning.

(TONE)

Q: Why did they decide to see the movie again?

A. They like watching movies twice.

B. They missed the beginning of the movie.

C. They didn't find the theater after all.

D. They didn't like that movie very much.

* *lose one's way* 迷路

49. (**C**) Ann took a long vacation, and now she is on her way to Thailand. Her flight leaves Tokyo at 10:30 in the morning, and makes a stop in Hong Kong for a couple of hours. She arrives in Bangkok at 5:30 in the evening.

(TONE)

Q: How long does Ann have to wait in Hong Kong?

A. For her long vacation.

B. At 10:30 in the next morning.

C. For a couple of hours.

D. For about seven hours.

* *on one's way to* 往~的途中

50. (**C**) This is the final call for passengers on Northwest Airlines Flight 006 to Detroit, Taipei and Singapore. The flight is now boarding at Gate 13 and is due to depart in ten minutes. Would any passengers who have not yet boarded please proceed as quickly as possible to Gate 13 for immediate boarding?

(TONE)

Q: Which gate is the flight departing from?

A. 6.　　　　　　　　B. 10.

C. 13.　　　　　　　 D. 30.

* due ﹝ dju ﹞ *adj.* 預定的　　depart ﹝ dɪ'pɑrt ﹞ *v.* 離開
proceed ﹝ prə'sid ﹞ *v.* 前進

51. (**C**) We regret to announce that the main elevators are temporarily out of order. Customers are kindly requested to use the stairs or escalators. Disabled customers are advised to contact our floor staff who will show them to the service elevator. We apologize for any inconvenience.

(TONE)

Q: Where was this announcement probably made?

A. At an airport.　　　　　B. At a hospital.

C. In a department store.　 D. At a school.

* temporarily ﹝'tɛmpə,rɛrəlɪ﹞ *adv.* 暫時地　　*out of order* 故障的
escalator ﹝'ɛskə,letə﹞ *n.* 電扶梯　　staff ﹝ stæf ﹞ *n.* 全體職員
service elevator 員工（送貨）電梯

52. (**A**) The outlook for tomorrow calls for cloudy skies in the morning, giving way to clear skies in the afternoon. Tomorrow's high will be 26 degrees centigrade, with a 40% chance of rain before noon. The low tonight will be 18 degrees.

(TONE)
Q: What is the chance of rain before noon?
A. 40%.
B. 14%.
C. 20%.
D. 26%.

* outlook (ˈaʊtˌlʊk) n. (未來) 天氣情勢
centigrade (ˈsɛntəˌgred) adj. 攝氏的

53. (**B**) Due to the avalanche earlier this morning, all the runs on the upper slopes will be closed for the rest of the day. Furthermore, the cable car will stop running at 12:30 this afternoon, due to expected high winds.

(TONE)
Q: What sport is this announcement concerned with?
A. Mountain climbing.
B. Skiing.
C. Car racing.
D. Windsurfing.

* *due to* 由於~　　avalanche (ˈævəˌlæntʃ) n. 雪崩
run (rʌn) n. 路線　　upper (ˈʌpɚ) adj. 上面的
slope (slop) n. 坡　　*cable car* 纜車
windsurfing (ˈwɪndˌsɝfɪŋ) n. 風浪板運動

54. (**A**) It looks like we're going to have another beautiful day in Long Beach and the surrounding area.　Temperatures will be in the low- to mid-seventies with a high around seventy-six.

(TONE)
Q: Where will it be sunny and warm?
A. In Long Beach.
B. In Sandy Head.
C. In Cape Hook.
D. In Silver Cup.

55. (**B**) As a result of the icy road conditions tonight, there have been a number of traffic accidents in the city and surrounding suburbs.　Consequently, traffic has been very slow in center city and most of the outlying areas.

(TONE)
Q: Why has traffic been so slow?
A. One of the major highways was shut down.
B. There have been many traffic accidents.
C. A lot of the roads are being repaired.
D. Due to rain, many roads are flooded.

　　* icy ('aɪsɪ) *adj.* 結冰的　　outlying ('aʊt,laɪɪŋ) *adj.* 外圍的

56. (**A**) In accepting this award, I want to thank the people who worked behind the scenes.　I especially want to thank Jeffrey Wheeler for his fund-raising efforts and Marianne Burke for getting approval from city council.　We couldn't have done it without your expertise as well as your enthusiasm.

(TONE)

Q: Why is the man making a speech?

A. He has been given an award.

B. He is presenting an award.

C. He is trying to raise money.

D. He is trying to get support.

* **behind the scenes** 在幕後 fund-raising (ˈfʌndˌrezɪŋ) *adj.* 募款的
approval (əˈpruvḷ) *n.* 認可 **city council** 市議會
expertise (ˌɛkspɚˈtiz) *n.* 專門知識

57. (**D**) One of the first domesticated animals was the horse. Horses
were prized for their strength, and their ability to run for long
distances at great speeds. The first horse we know of, the
Eohippus, lived over 40 million years ago. It was small, and
a little like a dog.

(TONE)

Q: How long have horses been in existence?

A. Several million years.

B. 10 million years.

C. 40 million years.

D. Over 40 million years.

* domesticated (dəˈmɛstəˌketɪd) *adj.* 馴養的
Eohippus (ˌioˈhɪpəs) *n.* 始祖馬

58. (**C**) Jack London was born in San Francisco California, on January
12, 1876. After spending his childhood on California ranches
and the streets of Oakland, he experienced countless jobs: he
became a sailor, a worker at a canning factory, a jute mill,
a laundry, and so on.

(TONE)

Q: Where was London born?

A. In the Far North.

B. In Oakland.

C. In San Francisco.

D. In New York.

* ranch〔 ræntʃ 〕 *n.* 大牧場　　***canning factory*** 食品裝罐場
jute〔 dʒut 〕 *n.* 黃麻　　laundry〔 'lɔndrɪ 〕 *n.* 洗衣店

59. (**C**) Outdated weather equipment is to blame for the lack of an
early warning before several killer tornadoes hit the Tampa
Bay area.　The chief meteorologist, Robert Balfour, said
that the current technology is definitely archaic.　It wasn't
designed to detect tornadoes as they developed, he said.　It
was designed to detect rainfall.

(TONE)

Q: Why was there no warning about the tornadoes?

A. The weather equipment was destroyed by the storms.

B. Heavy rain damaged the weather equipment.

C. The weather equipment was not able to pick up developing
tornadoes.

D. Nobody could operate the new weather equipment properly.

* outdated〔 ‚aʊt'detɪd 〕 *adj.* 舊式的
weather equipment 氣象儀器
meteorologist〔 ‚mitɪə'rɑlədʒɪst 〕 *n.* 氣象學者
archaic〔 ɑr'keɪk 〕 *adj.* 古式的　　detect〔 dɪ'tɛkt 〕 *v.* 偵察
tornado〔 tɔr'nedo 〕 *n.* 龍捲風　　***pick up*** 接收

60. (**B**) Are you a regular smoker?　Then, you are probably losing about 5 ½ minutes of life expectancy for each cigarette you smoke.　Up to age 65, people who smoke 20 or more cigarettes a day are said to die at almost twice the rate for nonsmokers in the same age group.

(TONE)

Q: What is the risk of death for people who smoke over 20 cigarettes a day?

A. Half the risk for nonsmokers.
B. Double the risk for nonsmokers.
C. Five and a half times the risk for nonsmokers.
D. 85 percent of the risk for nonsmokers.

* *life expectancy* 平均壽命

English Listening Comprehension Test

Test Book No. 15

This listening comprehension test will test your ability to understand spoken English. In this test, each conversation, statement and question will be spoken JUST ONE TIME. They will not be written out for you. There are four parts to this test. Special instructions will be given to you at the beginning of each part.

Part A

In Part A, you will see several pictures in your test book. For each picture, you will be asked 1 to 3 questions. For each question, you will hear four possible answers. Choose the best answer according to what you see in the picture.

Example:

You will see:

You will hear: What is this?
A. This is a table.
B. This is a chair.
C. This is a watch.
D. This is a doll.

The best answer to the question "What is this?" is B: "This is a chair." Therefore, you should choose answer B.

A. Questions 1-4

B. Questions 5-7

C. Questions 8-10

D. Questions 11-13

E. Questions 14-15

Part B

In Part B, you will hear 15 questions. After you hear a question, read the four possible answers in your test book and decide which one is the best answer to the question you have heard.

Example:

> You will hear: What does your father do?
>
> You will read: A. He's 50 years old.
> B. He's a teacher.
> C. He's hungry.
> D. He's in Los Angeles.

The best answer to the question "What does your father do?" is B: "He's a teacher." Therefore, you should choose answer B.

Please go to the next page. ⇨

16. A. No, you weren't.
　　 B. Yes, you were.
　　 C. Yes, I was.
　　 D. No, I was.

17. A. Sure, I don't.
　　 B. No, she speaks too fast.
　　 C. Yes, please.
　　 D. All right.

18. A. Yes, I'd like to.
　　 B. Yes, I like it.
　　 C. No, I wouldn't like.
　　 D. Do you have enough time?

19. A. Yes, a medium cola,
　　　 please.
　　 B. Yes, you are boring.
　　 C. Yes, these are on sale.
　　 D. Yes, I want to.

20. A. Much better, thanks.
　　 B. I feel you're right.
　　 C. I don't feel like taking
　　　 a walk now.
　　 D. This cloth feels soft.

21. A. For two o'clock.
　　 B. For two hours.
　　 C. Yes, I have watched it.
　　 D. About one o'clock.

22. A. The one without chemicals is.
　　 B. I know.　Ants hate clean
　　　 places.
　　 C. We changed our minds.
　　 D. How's everything?

23. A. If I knew, I would tell
　　　 you where she lives.
　　 B. She had told me where she
　　　 lives two days ago.
　　 C. If I were you, I would be
　　　 angry.
　　 D. If I had told you where she
　　　 lives, she would be angry.

24. A. It really doesn't matter.
　　 B. Yes, thank you.
　　 C. Yes, I'd like to buy these
　　　 things.
　　 D. I'm sorry.　This jelly is
　　　 too old.

25. A. I have only one truck.
    B. I will give you five.
    C. The more, the better.
    D. I need a lot of time.

26. A. I know milk shakes will make you tired.
    B. I know milk shakes will make you fat.
    C. I know milk shakes will make you hungry.
    D. I know milk shakes will make you wait.

27. A. So has mine.
    B. Mine does, too.
    C. But mine hasn't.
    D. Mine doesn't, either.

28. A. He's on English lesson.
    B. He's not studying lesson nine.
    C. He's on Lesson Ten.
    D. Lesson Eight is quite easy.

29. A. No, I told you nothing.
    B. No, no.
    C. Thank you, too.
    D. You are welcome.

30. A. Yes, I have a new computer.
    B. Yes, I'd like to buy one.
    C. Yes, I'll use it tomorrow.
    D. Yes, it helps a lot.

Part C

In Part C, you will hear 15 conversations between a man and a woman. After each conversation, you will hear a question about the conversation. After you hear the question, read the four possible answers in your test book and choose the best answer to the question you have heard.

Example:

You will hear:　(Man)　　　How do you go to school every day?
　　　　　　　(Woman)　　Usually by bus. Sometimes by taxi.

　　　　　　　TONE:　　　How does the woman go to school?

You will read:　A. She always goes to school on foot.
　　　　　　　B. She usually takes a bike.
　　　　　　　C. She takes either a bus or a taxi.
　　　　　　　D. She usually goes to school by bus, never by taxi.

The best answer to the question "How does the woman go to school?" is C: "She takes either a bus or a taxi." Therefore, you should choose answer C.

Please go to the next page. ⇨

31. A. She is pleased to know
    about their moving.
   B. Moving to the east is better
    than to the west.
   C. Probably she will be
    content.
   D. She is a little disappointed.

32. A. The man got the flu.
   B. The woman went to school.
   C. Many students caught the
    flu.
   D. The junior high school was
    over earlier than usual.

33. A. Be ready for a panel
    discussion.
   B. Choose a topic and write
    a research paper.
   C. Read an assignment for
    two hours.
   D. Read chapters and
    summarize them.

34. A. Jim always plays at about
    the same level.
   B. Jim is very defensive.
   C. Jim plays a fair game.
   D. Jim's game is artificial.

35. A. That he's prepared for it.
   B. That it will be difficult.
   C. That he missed it.
   D. That it's hopeless to study
    for it.

36. A. Deliver the freezer.
   B. Defrost the meat.
   C. Obey the law.
   D. Freeze the meat.

37. A. She had already seen it.
   B. Her cousin paid her a visit.
   C. Her cousin stopped to buy
    something.
   D. Her watch stopped and she
    didn't know the time.

38. A. Apologetic.
    B. Angry.
    C. Annoyed.
    D. Disappointed.

39. A. He prefers his old set of
       clubs.
    B. He has little chance to
       play golf.
    C. He's playing better golf
       recently.
    D. He's too old to play much
       golf.

40. A. On a farm.
    B. In a slaughterhouse.
    C. In a market.
    D. In a convenience store.

41. A. In a taxi.
    B. On a bus.
    C. In an elevator.
    D. On a train.

42. A. In a hospital.
    B. In a beauty parlor.
    C. In a classroom.
    D. In a hotel room.

43. A. He is worried because
       he left his key.
    B. He took the wrong train.
    C. He lost his bike.
    D. He arrived at the office late.

44. A. She doesn't like funny
       horror movies.
    B. She's met a movie star
       recently.
    C. She would take action
       right away.
    D. She saw a comedian last
       Sunday.

45. A. 12 years.
    B. 11 years.
    C. A few days.
    D. A couple of weeks.

Part D

In Part D, you will hear 15 short talks. After each talk, you will hear a question about the talk. After you hear the question, read the four possible answers in your test book and choose the best answer to the question you have heard.

Example:

You will hear: Well, that's all for Unit 15. For today's homework, please do the review questions on page 80, and we'll check the answers tomorrow. Now, let's go on to Unit 16.

TONE: What is the teacher going to do next in today's class?

You will read: A. Check the homework.
B. Review Unit 15.
C. Start a new unit.
D. Answer students' questions.

The best answer to the question "What is the teacher going to do next in today's class?" is C: "Start a new unit."   Therefore, you should choose answer C.

Please go to the next page. ⇨

46. A. To keep the weather very hot.
    B. To use less water.
    C. To use large amounts of water.
    D. To be very careful about the weather.

47. A. To rent a van.
    B. To go to a campground.
    C. To break down.
    D. To continue their vacation.

48. A. It has mild weather, good food, and jobs.
    B. There is plenty of work for farmers.
    C. Many airlines fly to and from this city.
    D. Frequent rain means lots of drinking water.

49. A. Big and quiet.
    B. Next to the station.
    C. Convenient but noisy.
    D. Not so convenient as the old one.

50. A. One a day.
    B. Two a day.
    C. One every other day.
    D. One a week.

51. A. Around the beginning of the century.
    B. In the 1920s.
    C. In the 1950s.
    D. This information is not given in the announcement.

52. A. Use public transportation.
    B. Take the Dock Street exit.
    C. Not use Franklin Pike or Madison Blvd.
    D. Not use the expressway.

53. A. Panicked.
    B. Left the ERM.
    C. Stabilized their currencies.
    D. Unified their markets.

54. A. Partly cloudy with a high of 60.
    B. Sunny with a high around 76.
    C. A 60 percent chance of rain.
    D. Rain with a high of 60.

55. A. 1:40 a.m.
    B. 8 p.m.
    C. 8 a.m.
    D. 9 p.m.

56. A. Five for a dollar.
    B. Twenty-nine cents a
       pound.
    C. Fifty-nine cents a pound.
    D. The speaker doesn't say.

57. A. They exercised a lot.
    B. They pulled many chariots.
    C. Through evolution.
    D. Men helped them to
       strengthen their legs.

58. A. In 1835.
    B. In 1935.
    C. In 1875.
    D. In 1895.

59. A. The trains arrived several
       hours late.
    B. Taxi drivers staged a
       demonstration.
    C. There was a serious traffic
       accident.
    D. Railway workers went on
       strike.

60. A. 5%.
    B. 10%.
    C. 25%.
    D. 50%.

Listening Test 15 詳解

Part A

For questions number 1 to 4, please look at picture A.

1. (**A**) Question number 1, what is the man in the left room on the second floor doing?

    A. He is stealing.   B. He is smoking.

    C. He is exercising.   D. He is playing.

2. (**C**) Question number 2, please look at picture A again. What is the man in the right room on the second floor doing?

    A. He is reading.   B. He is sleeping.

    C. He is proposing.   D. He is exercising.

    * propose (prə'poz) v. 求婚

3. (**D**) Question number 3, please look at picture A again. What are the four men on the first floor doing?

    A. They are playing music.

    B. They are playing mahjong.

    C. They are playing video games.

    D. They are playing cards.

    * mahjong (ma'dʒɑŋ) n. 麻將   *video games* 電動玩具

    play cards 玩撲克牌

4. (**A**) Question number 4, please look at picture A again. What is the man in the room on the right on the first floor doing?

    A. He is lifting weights.

    B. He is playing cards.

    C. He is watching TV.

    D. He is reading.

    * *lift weights* 舉重

For questions number 5 to 7, please look at picture B.

5. (**C**) Question number 5, what is the young boy riding?
   A. He is riding a bicycle.
   B. He is riding a roller-skate.
   C. He is riding a skateboard.
   D. He is riding a motorcycle.
   * roller-skate ('rolə,sket) *n.* 輪式溜冰鞋
     skateboard ('sket,bord) *n.* 滑板

6. (**D**) Question number 6, please look at picture B again. What are the two men doing?
   A. They are playing a guitar and a hat.
   B. They are playing a violin and a guitar.
   C. They are playing a tambourine and a violin.
   D. They are playing a guitar and a tambourine.
   * violin (,vaɪə'lin) *n.* 小提琴   tambourine (,tæmbə'rin) *n.* 鈴鼓

7. (**C**) Question number 7, please look at picture B again. What is the woman doing?
   A. She is shopping.
   B. She is walking a cat.
   C. She is littering.
   D. She is singing.
   * litter ('lɪtə) *v.* 亂丟 (垃圾)

For questions number 8 to 10, please look at picture C.

8. (**C**) Question number 8, what is the woman making?
   A. She is making fried noodles.
   B. She is making pizza.
   C. She is making soup.
   D. She is making a cake.
   * *fried noodles* 炒麵

9. (**C**) Question number 9, please look at picture C again.　Where is the woman cooking on?

 A. She is cooking on the oven.

 B. She is cooking on the sink.

 C. She is cooking on the stove.

 D. She is cooking on the refrigerator.

 * oven〔ˋʌvən〕*n.* 烤箱　　sink〔sɪŋk〕*n.* 洗手台
 stove〔stov〕*n.* 爐子

10. (**D**) Question number 10, please look at picture C again.　What is the man holding?

 A. He is holding a plate.

 B. He is holding a cup.

 C. He is holding a bowl.

 D. He is holding a jar.

 * plate〔plet〕*n.* 盤子　　bowl〔bol〕*n.* 碗　　jar〔dʒɑr〕*n.* 廣口瓶

For questions number 11 to 13, please look at picture D.

11. (**A**) Question number 11, what is this a picture of?

 A. It is a post office.

 B. It is a police station.

 C. It is a market.

 D. It is a bank.

12. (**C**) Question number 12, please look at picture D again.　What is the woman with dark hair doing?

 A. She is mailing a parcel.

 B. She is waiting in line.

 C. She is mailing a letter.

 D. She is weighing a package.

 * parcel〔ˋpɑrsl̩〕*n.* 小包　　*wait in line* 排隊等候
 weigh〔we〕*v.* 稱重

13. (**B**) Question number 13, please look at picture D again. How many people are in line at the window on the left?
    A. One.
    B. Two.
    C. Three.
    D. None.

For questions number 14 to 15, please look at picture E.

14. (**C**) Question number 14, what is the gorilla holding?
    A. It is holding a hat.
    B. It is holding a bag.
    C. It is holding an umbrella.
    D. It is holding a woman.
    * gorilla (gəˈrɪlə) *n.* 大猩猩

15. (**D**) Question number 15, please look at picture E again.   Where is the woman?
    A. She is under a hat.
    B. She is in the closet.
    C. She is on a shelf.
    D. She is behind a counter.
    * closet (ˈklɑzɪt) *n.* 櫥櫃   shelf (ʃɛlf) *n.* 架子
    counter (ˈkaʊntɚ) *n.* 櫃檯

Part B

16. (**C**) Weren't you busy yesterday?
    A. No, you weren't.
    B. Yes, you were.
    C. Yes, I was.
    D. No, I was.

17. (**B**) Don't you understand Mary's English?

    A. Sure, I don't.

    B. No, she speaks too fast.

    C. Yes, please.

    D. All right.

18. (**A**) Would you like to go shopping tomorrow?

    A. Yes, I'd like to.

    B. Yes, I like it.

    C. No, I wouldn't like.

    D. Do you have enough time?

19. (**A**) May I help you, sir?

    A. Yes, a medium cola, please.

    B. Yes, you are boring.

    C. Yes, these are on sale.

    D. Yes, I want to.

    * medium ('midɪəm) *adj.* 中杯的   cola ('kolə) *n.* 可樂

      on sale 大拍賣

20. (**A**) How do you feel today, Mark?

    A. Much better, thanks.

    B. I feel you're right.

    C. I don't feel like taking a walk now.

    D. This cloth feels soft.

    * feel (fil) *v.* 覺得；摸起來   cloth (klɔθ) *n.* 布

21. (**B**) How long have you watched TV?

    A. For two o'clock.

    B. For two hours.

    C. Yes, I have watched it.

    D. About one o'clock.

22. (**A**) Do you know which brand is better?
　　A. The one without chemicals is.
　　B. I know.　Ants hate clean places.
　　C. We changed our minds.
　　D. How's everything?
　　* brand (brænd) *n.* 品牌　　chemical ('kɛmɪkl̩) *n.* 化學藥品；農藥
　　ant (ænt) *n.* 螞蟻

23. (**A**) Please tell me where she lives.
　　A. If I knew, I would tell you where she lives.
　　B. She had told me where she lives two days ago.
　　C. If I were you, I would be angry.
　　D. If I had told you where she lives, she would be angry.

24. (**C**) May I help you?
　　A. It really doesn't matter.
　　B. Yes, thank you.
　　C. Yes, I'd like to buy these things.
　　D. I'm sorry.　This jelly is too old.
　　* jelly ('dʒɛlɪ) *n.* 果凍

25. (**C**) How many do you need?
　　A. I have only one truck.　　B. I will give you five.
　　C. The more, the better.　　D. I need a lot of time.
　　* *The more, the better.* 愈多愈好。

26. (**B**) Okay.　Let's eat there, but no milk shakes!
　　A. I know milk shakes will make you tired.
　　B. I know milk shakes will make you fat.
　　C. I know milk shakes will make you hungry.
　　D. I know milk shakes will make you wait.
　　* *milk shake* 奶昔

27. (**B**) My father works hard.
    - A. So has mine.
    - B. Mine does, too.
    - C. But mine hasn't.
    - D. Mine doesn't, either.

28. (**C**) What lesson is he on?
    - A. He's on English lesson.
    - B. He's not studying lesson nine.
    - C. He's on Lesson Ten.
    - D. Lesson Eight is quite easy.

    * *What lesson is he on*? 他在上第幾課？

29. (**D**) Jack, thank you for telling us the news.
    - A. No, I told you nothing.
    - B. No, no.
    - C. Thank you, too.
    - D. You are welcome.

30. (**D**) Kevin, do you often use this new computer?
    - A. Yes, I have a new computer.
    - B. Yes, I'd like to buy one.
    - C. Yes, I'll use it tomorrow.
    - D. Yes, it helps a lot.

Part C

31. (**D**) M: Are you disappointed that they're moving to the west?
    W: Perhaps in some ways.

    (TONE)
    Q: What does the woman mean?
    - A. She is pleased to know about their moving.
    - B. Moving to the east is better than to the west.
    - C. Probably she will be content.
    - D. She is a little disappointed.

    * *in some ways* 在某些方面   content〔kən'tɛnt〕*adj.* 滿足的

32. (**C**)　W: I was surprised to see you with your family at the Shopping
　　　　　　　Mall yesterday.
　　　　　　M: Our junior high school was closed down because a flu
　　　　　　　broke out.

　　　　　(TONE)
　　　　　Q: What happened yesterday?
　　　　　A. The man got the flu.
　　　　　B. The woman went to school.
　　　　　C. Many students caught the flu.
　　　　　D. The junior high school was over earlier than usual.

　　　　　* flu〔flu〕*n.* 流行性感冒　　***break out*** 爆發

33. (**D**)　W: I was absent from biology class today.　Is there any
　　　　　　　assignment for next week?
　　　　　　M: Yes, we have to read 5 chapters in the book the professor
　　　　　　　assigned and write a two-page summary.

　　　　　(TONE)
　　　　　Q: What have these students been asked to do before next class?
　　　　　A. Be ready for a panel discussion.
　　　　　B. Choose a topic and write a research paper.
　　　　　C. Read an assignment for two hours.
　　　　　D. Read chapters and summarize them.

　　　　　* chapter〔'tʃæptɚ〕*n.* 章　　summary〔'sʌmərɪ〕*n.* 摘要
　　　　　panel discussion 小組討論會
　　　　　summarize〔'sʌmə,raɪz〕*v.* 扼要說明；概述

34. (**A**)　W: I saw your brother Jim in the basketball game yesterday.
　　　　　　　What a brilliant basketball player he is!
　　　　　　M: Well, actually he isn't, but his game is very consistent.

(TONE)

Q: What does the man mean?

A. Jim always plays at about the same level.

B. Jim is very defensive.

C. Jim plays a fair game.

D. Jim's game is artificial.

* brilliant ('brɪljənt) *adj.* 出色的
consistent (kən'sɪstənt) *adj.* 前後一致的
level ('lɛvḷ) *n.* 水準　defensive (dɪ'fɛnsɪv) *adj.* 防禦的
artificial (ˌɑrtə'fɪʃəl) *adj.* 不自然的

35. (**B**) M: I'm really worried about passing the exam tomorrow.

W: It's too late to worry about it now, Joe.

(TONE)

Q: What does Joe think about the exam?

A. That he's prepared for it.

B. That it will be difficult.

C. That he missed it.

D. That it's hopeless to study for it.

36. (**B**) W: You didn't take the meat out of the freezer in advance.

M: That's no crime.　We'll just wait for it to thaw and eat it later.

(TONE)

Q: What did the man neglect to do?

A. Deliver the freezer.

B. Defrost the meat.

C. Obey the law.

D. Freeze the meat.

* meat (mit) *n.* 肉　freezer ('frizɚ) *n.* 冷凍庫
crime (kraɪm) *n.* 愚昧或錯誤的行爲　　thaw (θɔ) *v.* 融化；解凍
defrost (aɪ'frɔst) *v.* 解凍

37. (**B**) M: Did you see the science fiction movie on television last night?

W: I would have watched it, but my cousin stopped by for a visit. I hadn't seen her for more than a year.

(TONE)

Q: Why didn't the woman watch the movie last night?

A. She had already seen it.

B. Her cousin paid her a visit.

C. Her cousin stopped to buy something.

D. Her watch stopped and she didn't know the time.

* *science fiction movie* 科幻電影

38. (**C**) M: Would you mind turning down your stereo?

W: I'm sorry, but I can't hear you.

M: I asked if you would turn down the music. It's too loud.

(TONE)

Q: How does the man feel?

A. Apologetic.

B. Angry.

C. Annoyed.

D. Disappointed.

* *turn down* 關小聲　　stereo ('stɛrɪo) *n.* 音響
apologetic (ə,pɑlə'dʒɛtɪk) *adj.* 道歉的
annoyed (ə'nɔɪd) *adj.* 覺得煩的

39. (**C**) W: Hi, Bill. Have you been playing much golf lately?

M: Hello, Joan. I play as often as I can get out of the house. And by the way, I have a new set of clubs. They seem to have helped my game, though they're much heavier than my old set.

(TONE)

Q: What does Bill tell Joan?

A. He prefers his old set of clubs.

B. He has little chance to play golf.

C. He's playing better golf recently.

D. He's too old to play much golf.

* golf〔gɑlf〕*n.* 高爾夫球　***a set of*** 一套~
club〔klʌb〕*n.* 高爾夫球具

40. (**A**) W: These hogs look fine! Are you raising them for market?

M: Not this year. With the cost of feed and the low profit, it doesn't seem worthwhile. I'll just slaughter them for my own consumption.

(TONE)

Q: Where did this conversation probably occur?

A. On a farm.

B. In a slaughterhouse.

C. In a market.

D. In a convenience store.

* hog〔hɑg〕*n.* 豬　raise〔rez〕*v.* 飼養　feed〔fid〕*n.* 飼料
slaughter〔'slɔtɚ〕*v.* 屠宰　consumption〔kən'sʌmpʃən〕*n.* 消耗；吃喝
slaughterhouse〔'slɔtɚ,haʊs〕*n.* 屠宰場

41. (**C**) M: What floor is the Colfax Corporation on?

W: I think Colfax is on the second. We just passed it.

M: Oh, I'll have to wait until we go down.

(TONE)

Q: Where are they?

A. In a taxi.　　　　　B. On a bus.

C. In an elevator.　　　D. On a train.

* elevator〔'ɛlə,vetɚ〕*n.* 電梯

42. (**D**)　W: Here is your room, sir.　I'm sure you'll enjoy this
　　　　　　　spectacular view of the ocean.
　　　　　　M: Thank you.　Here's a tip.　Keep the change.
　　　　　　W: Thank you, sir.　If there is anything you need to know,
　　　　　　　please call me at any time.　I'll be in the lobby all night.

　　　　　(TONE)
　　　　　Q: Where does this conversation take place?
　　　　　A. In a hospital.
　　　　　B. In a beauty parlor.
　　　　　C. In a classroom.
　　　　　D. In a hotel room.

　　　　　* spectacular〔spɛk'tækjələ〕*adj.* 壯觀的　　　tip〔tɪp〕*n.* 小費
　　　　　　Keep the change. 不用找了。　　***beauty parlor*** 美容院

43. (**A**)　M: Damn it!　I forgot to bring the key to my bike.　I left it at
　　　　　　　the office.
　　　　　　W: Why don't you go back and get it?
　　　　　　M: Then, I'll miss the last train.　I only have 5 minutes.

　　　　　(TONE)
　　　　　Q: Why is the man upset?
　　　　　A. He is worried because he left his key.
　　　　　B. He took the wrong train.
　　　　　C. He lost his bike.
　　　　　D. He arrived at the office late.

　　　　　Damn it! 該死！　　upset〔ʌp'sɛt〕*adj.* 不高興的

44. (**A**)　W: Seen any good movies lately?
　　　　　　M: I saw a comedy type of horror movie last Sunday.　It was
　　　　　　　so funny.　You should see it.
　　　　　　W: Oh, I'd rather go to an action movie than something like that.

(TONE)

Q: What does the woman mean?

A. She doesn't like funny horror movies.

B. She's met a movie star recently.

C. She would take action right away.

D. She saw a comedian last Sunday.

* lately (ˈletlɪ) *adv.* 最近 　　comedy (ˈkɑmədɪ) *n.* 喜劇
  horror movie 恐怖片 　　*action movie* 動作片
  take action 採取行動 　　comedian (kəˈmidɪən) *n.* 喜劇演員

45. (**C**) W: I'll be transferred to Miami in two weeks.

M: Have you ever been there before?

W: Yes, about twelve years ago, but only for a couple of days.

(TONE)

Q: How long was she in Miami?

A. 12 years. 　　　　　　B. 11 years.

C. A few days. 　　　　　D. A couple of weeks.

* transfer (trænsˈfɝ) *v.* 調職 　　*a couple of* 幾個

Part D

46. (**B**) Last summer was troublesome in Japan because of the hot weather and little rain. The water shortage worried many people. Around the country people were required to use less water.

(TONE)

Q: What were people required to do last summer?

A. To keep the weather very hot.

B. To use less water.

C. To use large amounts of water.

D. To be very careful about the weather.

* troublesome (ˈtrʌblsəm) *adj.* 麻煩的 　　shortage (ˈʃɔrtɪdʒ) *n.* 缺乏

47. (**A**)　The Hendersons wanted to go to a campground in their own car.　But the engine overheated and broke down.　They were forced to rent a van in order to continue with their vacation.

(TONE)
Q: What were the Hendersons forced to do?
A. To rent a van.
B. To go to a campground.
C. To break down.
D. To continue their vacation.

* campground (ˈkæmp͵graʊnd) *n.* 營地　　overheat (ˈovəˈhit) *v.* 過熱
  break down 故障　　***be forced to*** 被迫　　van (væn) *n.* 箱型車

48. (**A**)　Seattle, Washington is one of the fastest-growing cities in the U.S.A.　The weather may be rainy, but the temperature is never too hot or too cold.　The public market downtown always has fresh fish, vegetables, and fruit.　Thanks to the aircraft and software industries, there are plenty of jobs.

(TONE)
Q: Why is Seattle a good place to live?
A. It has mild weather, good food, and jobs.
B. There is plenty of work for farmers.
C. Many airlines fly to and from this city.
D. Frequent rain means lots of drinking water.

* aircraft (ˈɛr͵kræft) *n.* 飛機　　software (ˈsɔft͵wɛr) *n.* (電腦) 軟體
  mild (maɪld) *adj.* 溫和的　　airline (ˈɛr͵laɪn) *n.* 航空公司

49. (**C**)　Tom moved into a new apartment last week.　It's a lot more convenient than his old place.　He can walk to the station in five minutes, and there are many stores in the neighborhood. However, it's noisy around his apartment.

(TONE)

Q: How is Tom's new apartment?

A. Big and quiet. 　　　　　　B. Next to the station.

C. Convenient but noisy.

D. Not so convenient as the old one.

50. (**A**) Between October 1st and November 30th, passengers on any of our daily flights to London's Heathrow can look forward to some unbelievable offers.　Fifty percent off on a huge selection of top London hotels, a free champagne dinner on arrival at the hotel of your choice, complimentary theater tickets, department store discount tickets, and free sightseeing tours.

(TONE)

Q: How many flights does this airline have to London?

A. One a day. 　　　　　　　　B. Two a day.

C. One every other day. 　　　　D. One a week.

* ***look forward to*** 期待　　champagne (ʃæm'pen) *n.* 香檳
complimentary (ˌkɑmplə'mɛntərɪ) *adj.* 免費的
discount tickets 折扣券　　flight (flaɪt) *n.* 班機

51. (**C**) We're sorry to announce to all you eager baseball fans out there that the game between the Salt Lake Giants and the Chicago Redcats has been rained out.　In its place, KCTV is showing the '50s classic *Big Joe* starring Clark Westwood.

(TONE)

Q: When was the movie *Big Joe* made?

A. Around the beginning of the century.

B. In the 1920s. 　　　　　　　C. In the 1950s.

D. This information is not given in the announcement.

* eager ('igɚ) *adj.* 急切的　　fan (fæn) *n.* 球迷
be rained out 因雨中止；延期　　classic ('klæsɪk) *n.* 經典名著
star (stɑr) *v.* 由～主演

52. (**D**) On the Cross-town Expressway, traffic is finally moving again
after a three-hour delay due to an overturned tractor-trailer
blocking the Dock Street exit. In order to avoid further
delays, I would advise all travelers returning home from center
city to use Franklin Pike or Madison Boulevard.

(TONE)
Q: What should drivers do to avoid further delays?
A. Use public transportation.
B. Take the Dock Street exit.
C. Not use Franklin Pike or Madison Blvd.
D. Not use the expressway.

* expressway (ɪk'sprɛs,we) *n.* 高速道路
   overturned ('ovɚ,tɝnd) *adj.* 翻覆的   tractor ('træktɚ) *n.* 牽引機
   trailer ('trelɚ) *n.* 拖車   exit ('ɛksɪt) *n.* 出口
   pike (paɪk) *n.* 高速收費道路   boulevard ('bulə,vɑrd) *n.* 林蔭大道

53. (**B**) Recent events in the currency markets have caused a great deal
of panic. The United Kingdom and Italy, in a desperate bid to
stabilize their currencies, have left the ERM. In other words,
the whole issue of a unified European market is now in question,
and quite naturally, the U.S. government is very concerned.

(TONE)
Q: What have the U.K. and Italy done?
A. Panicked.
B. Left the ERM.
C. Stabilized their currencies.
D. Unified their markets.

* currency ('kɝənsɪ) *n.* 貨幣   panic ('pænɪk) *n.* 恐慌
   the United Kingdom 英國 (= *the U.K.*)
   issue ('ɪʃu) *n.* 問題   unified ('jnə,faɪd) *adj.* 聯合的
   in question 討論中   stabalize ('stæbl̩,aɪz) *v.* 使穩定

54. (**C**) The forecast for the western shores isn't entirely good, as a low-pressure system is rolling in from the west, with a sixty percent chance of rain for Cape Hook, Sandy Head, and Shipbottom Bay.

(TONE)
Q: What is the forecast for Shipbottom Bay?
A. Partly cloudy with a high of 60.
B. Sunny with a high around 76.
C. A 60 percent chance of rain.
D. Rain with a high of 60.

* forecast ('for,kæst) *n.* 預測　　*roll in* 大量湧進
chance of rain 降雨機率　　high (haɪ) *n.* 最高溫

55. (**B**) This emergency broadcast is a public service brought to you by channel 7 TV. The meteorological service has announced that hurricane Dan is moving toward Miami with speeds of up to 140 m.p.h., and is expected to hit land at about 8 o'clock tonight.

(TONE)
Q: When is the hurricane expected to hit land ?
A. 1:40 a.m.　　　　　B. 8 p.m.
C. 8 a.m.　　　　　　D. 9 p.m.

* emergency (ɪ'mɝdʒənsɪ) *n.* 緊急情況
broadcast ('brɔd,kæst) *n.* 廣播　　channel ('tʃænl̩) *n.* 頻道
meteorological (,mitɪərə'lɑdʒɪkl̩) *adj.* 氣象的
hurricane ('hɝɪ,ken) *n.* 颶風

56. (**D**) Bargains, bargains, bargains! At Mr. Green Gene's Farm Mart every last item has been marked down. That's right, low, low prices for you! We've got Idaho baking potatoes, only twenty-nine cents a pound; fresh Jersey tomatoes, five for a dollar; California strawberries, one pint for only fifty-nine cents.

(TONE)

Q: How much do the apples cost?

A. Five for a dollar.

B. Twenty-nine cents a pound.

C. Fifty-nine cents a pound.

D. The speaker doesn't say.

* bargain ('bɑrgɪn) *n.* 便宜貨　　item ('aɪtəm) *n.* 項目
  mark down 減價　　pint (paɪnt) *n.* 品脫 (= 0.47 公升)

57. (**C**) Horses developed strong legs in the course of their evolution.
Their strong legs helped them to escape prey.　Through
evolution, their toes developed into hooves.

(TONE)

Q: How did horses develop strong legs?

A. They exercised a lot.

B. They pulled many chariots.

C. Through evolution.

D. Men helped them to strengthen their legs.

* course (kors) *n.* 過程　　evolution (ˌɛvə'luʃən) *n.* 進化
  prey (pre) *n.* 捕食　　hoof (huf) *n.* 蹄 (複數為 *hooves*)
  chariot ('tʃærɪət) *n.* 四輪馬車　　strengthen ('strɛŋθən) *v.* 加強

58. (**A**) Mark Twain, or Samuel Clemens, was born in Florida, Missouri
in 1835.　In those days the Mississippi river was the route
connecting the nation's major cities, and it was Twain's
boyhood ambition to become a riverboat pilot.

(TONE)

Q: When was Mark Twain born?

A. In 1835.　　　　　B. In 1935.

C. In 1875.　　　　　D. In 1895.

* route (rut) *n.* 航線；路線　　pilot ('paɪlət) *n.* 舵手；領航員

59. (.**B**) And now for the local news.　Traffic was brought to a standstill in the city center for more than an hour this afternoon as over a hundred angry taxi drivers blocked streets with their cabs.

(TONE)

Q: What happened this afternoon?

A. The trains arrived several hours late.

B. Taxi drivers staged a demonstration.

C. There was a serious traffic accident.

D. Railway workers went on strike.

* standstill ('stænd,stɪl) n. 停滯　　block (blɑk) v. 阻塞
cab (kæb) n. 計程車　　*stage a demonstration* 發動示威
go on strike 進行罷工

60. (**C**) We can always use a new source of electricity.　At the present time, one-quarter of the world's electricity comes from dams and rivers.　Now scientists are learning how to use energy from the sea.　They are developing technology which can convert the force of waves into electricity.

(TONE)

Q: What percentage of electricity comes from dams and rivers?

A. 5 %.

B. 10 %.

C. 25 %.

D. 50 %.

* dam (dæm) n. 水壩　　convert (kən'vɝt) v. 轉變
percentage (pə'sɛntɪdʒ) n. 百分比

English Listening Comprehension Test

Test Book No. 16

This listening comprehension test will test your ability to understand spoken English. In this test, each conversation, statement and question will be spoken JUST ONE TIME. They will not be written out for you. There are four parts to this test. Special instructions will be given to you at the beginning of each part.

Part A

In Part A, you will see several pictures in your test book. For each picture, you will be asked 1 to 3 questions. For each question, you will hear four possible answers. Choose the best answer according to what you see in the picture.

Example:

You will see:

You will hear: What is this?
        A. This is a table.
        B. This is a chair.
        C. This is a watch.
        D. This is a doll.

The best answer to the question "What is this?" is B: "This is a chair." Therefore, you should choose answer B.

A. Questions 1-3

D. Questions 10-11

B. Questions 4-6

E. Questions 12-13

C. Questions 7-9

F. Questions 14-15

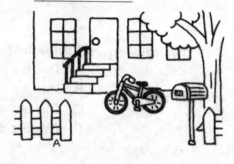

Part B

In Part B, you will hear 15 questions.   After you hear a question, read the four possible answers in your test book and decide which one is the best answer to the question you have heard.

Example:

<u>You will hear:</u>   What does your father do?

<u>You will read:</u>   A. He's 50 years old.
B. He's a teacher.
C. He's hungry.
D. He's in Los Angeles.

The best answer to the question "What does your father do?" is B: "He's a teacher."   Therefore, you should choose answer B.

Please go to the next page. ⇨

16. A. No, they are not interested.
    B. No, it is boring.
    C. Yes, it is interested.
    D. Yes, it is boring.

17. A. Yes, he is.
    B. Yes, it is.
    C. He is.
    D. No, he is.

18. A. Yes, I can speak neither.
    B. No, I can't speak neither
       of them.
    C. I can speak both of them.
    D. Either of them will do.

19. A. Sure.
    B. I don't like it very much.
    C. No, I don't.
    D. Yes, I like it very much.

20. A. Oh, it's nothing.
    B. Any time.
    C. I don't mind at all.
    D. Not bad.

21. A. Please do.
    B. Here you are.
    C. There it is.
    D. Here it is.

22. A. February 8, 1999.
    B. 9:22.
    C. Monday.
    D. Tomorrow morning.

23. A. By bus.
    B. For fun.
    C. The smaller one.
    D. A teacher.

24. A. It's not Jack, I am sure.
    B. It is my friend Tom that
       will come to see us.
    C. Jane likes to knock at
       someone's door.
    D. It must be Sue.

25. A. How nice it is!　Will you
　　　come with us?
　　B. We will have that for
　　　nothing.
　　C. You look great.
　　D. We will pay for that.

26. A. It is $3.00 every.
　　B. They are sold out.
　　C. They are $3.00 each.
　　　Children can get in at
　　　half price.
　　D. The tickets are on the desk.

27. A. Twice a week.
　　B. For two days.
　　C. Last week.
　　D. In my office.

28. A. What did you want?
　　B. I'm sorry you didn't
　　　like it.
　　C. I am glad you like it.
　　D. Was it a present?

29. A. That's all right.
　　B. Yes, she's very well.
　　C. It's all right.
　　D. Yes, she's very ill.

30. A. By bus.
　　B. I am a stranger here.
　　C. From China.
　　D. An American.

Part C

In Part C, you will hear 15 conversations between a man and a woman. After each conversation, you will hear a question about the conversation. After you hear the question, read the four possible answers in your test book and choose the best answer to the question you have heard.

Example:

You will hear: (Man)   How do you go to school every day?
               (Woman)   Usually by bus.   Sometimes by taxi.

               TONE: How does the woman go to school?

You will read: A. She always goes to school on foot.
               B. She usually takes a bike.
               C. She takes either a bus or a taxi.
               D. She usually goes to school by bus, never by taxi.

The best answer to the question "How does the woman go to school?" is C: "She takes either a bus or a taxi."   Therefore, you should choose answer C.

Please go to the next page. ⇨

31. A. She agrees with the man.
    B. She doesn't know the book.
    C. She likes the book very much.
    D. She doesn't know what to do.

32. A. She can go with him this
       afternoon.
    B. She has a lot to do today.
    C. She's almost as busy as he is.
    D. She might be finished by noon.

33. A. The man should buy a dif-
       ferent meal ticket each month.
    B. Individuals eat different
       amounts.
    C. Buying the meal ticket won't
       save the man money.
    D. The price of a meal varies
       from month to month.

34. A. Run in town.
    B. Look more carefully.
    C. Buying shoes from a catalogue.
    D. Find an easier place to exercise.

35. A. She doesn't like the
       professor very much.
    B. She doubts class will be
       canceled.
    C. She doesn't want to attend
       the conference.
    D. She wonders whether the
       professor is an accountant.

36. A. He doesn't expect to
       meet her at the seashore.
    B. He wants to know when
       she's coming.
    C. He wants to see how her
       experiment is progressing.
    D. He isn't interested in
       watching her.

37. A. Dan received them.
    B. Gloria forgot about them.
    C. Dan mailed them.
    D. Gloria has sent for them.

38. A. He's taller than anyone on campus.
    B. He's the best actor in the school.
    C. He's almost through with the campus tour.
    D. He's studying at college to be an actor.

39. A. She may need to take another course.
    B. The math course is too short.
    C. The graduation date has been changed.
    D. She should have gotten a better score.

40. A. Tea is better than coffee.
    B. The man should switch to tea.
    C. There are two reasons not to drink coffee.
    D. The man shouldn't drink either.

41. A. Accounting.
    B. Secretary.
    C. Sales.
    D. Guard.

42. A. An office worker.
    B. A police officer.
    C. A fellow passenger.
    D. A bell-hop.

43. A. For research.
    B. For pleasure.
    C. To see his family.
    D. For business.

44. A. Every week.
    B. Every month.
    C. Twice a month.
    D. Every other month.

45. A. Tom should quit smoking.
    B. Tom should buy cigarettes.
    C. Tom himself should think about where he smokes.
    D. Tom should go outside.

Part D

In Part D, you will hear 15 short talks. After each talk, you will hear a question about the talk. After you hear the question, read the four possible answers in your test book and choose the best answer to the question you have heard.

Example:

You will hear: Well, that's all for Unit 15. For today's homework, please do the review questions on page 80, and we'll check the answers tomorrow. Now, let's go on to Unit 16.

TONE: What is the teacher going to do next in today's class?

You will read: A. Check the homework.
                 B. Review Unit 15.
                 C. Start a new unit.
                 D. Answer students' questions.

The best answer to the question "What is the teacher going to do next in today's class?" is C: "Start a new unit." Therefore, you should choose answer C.

Please go to the next page. ⇨

46. A. He forgot to take pictures.
    B. He left it on the airplane.
    C. He bought it in Hawaii.
    D. Someone found it and sent it to him.

47. A. She damaged it slightly.
    B. She began driving it.
    C. She parked it at the supermarket.
    D. She damaged it seriously.

48. A. An hour early.
    B. To meet Jane.
    C. On Saturday.
    D. After her hiking trip with Jane.

49. A. On a train.
    B. On a plane.
    C. At a station.
    D. At Norfolk.

50. A. 1.1% less.
    B. 36% more.
    C. $86.4 billion more.
    D. 14.3% more.

51. A. Two days ago.
    B. Yesterday.
    C. This morning.
    D. This afternoon.

52. A. 277-9967.
    B. 276-2277.
    C. 277-7996.
    D. 279-7996.

53. A. At a university.
    B. At a high school.
    C. At a large corporation.
    D. In a government department.

54. A. Fifteen.
    B. Twenty-five.
    C. Fifty.
    D. Seventy-five.

55. A. Computers.
    B. Furniture.
    C. Lunch.
    D. Carpeting.

56. A. A movie that will be on
       television this weekend.
    B. A movie that starts showing
       soon at the theaters.
    C. A movie that has just come
       out on video.
    D. A movie that will be coming
       out on video soon.

57. A. Indonesia.
    B. Jakarta City.
    C. Batavia.
    D. Dutch East India.

58. A. It is usually cold in summer.
    B. It is usually warm in summer.
    C. It is both wet and cold in
       summer.
    D. It is rarely cold in summer.

59. A. Cigarette advertising.
    B. Government policies.
    C. Price increases for
       tobacco.
    D. Smoking-related
       diseases.

60. A. Cut the egg with a knife
       after cooking it.
    B. Turn the egg over while
       cooking it.
    C. Break the egg and poke
       the yolk before cooking it.
    D. Don't put the egg in a
       dish before cooking it.

Listening Test 16 詳解

Part A

For questions number 1 to 3, please look at picture A.

1. (**A**) Question number 1, where are these people?
  A. They are on a bus.　　B. They are in an office.
  C. They are in a hotel.　　D. They are in a department store.

2. (**B**) Question number 2, please look at picture A again.　What are the two standing girls doing?
  A. They are sitting on the bench.
  B. They are talking and reading.
  C. They are listening to music.
  D. They are sleeping.

3. (**C**) Question number 3, please look at picture A again.　Look at the person with the headset on.　What is he doing?
  A. He is watching his watch.
  B. He is thinking about smoking.
  C. He is listening to music.
  D. He is using a pocket electronic calculator.

  * headset ('hɛd,sɛt) *n.* 耳機　　pocket ('pakɪt) *adj.* 袖珍的
  electronic calculator 電子計算機

For questions number 4 to 6, please look at picture B.

4. (**C**) Question number 4, what is the boy on the right wearing on his head?
  A. He is riding a bicycle.
  B. He is wearing a pair of glasses.
  C. He is wearing a hat.
  D. He is wearing a shirt.

5. (**A**) Question number 5, please look at picture B again. What is
between the trees and the two boys?
   A. There is a bicycle.   B. There are hills.
   C. There are rabbits.   D. There are clouds.

6. (**B**) Question number 6, please look at picture B again. What can
you see in the sky?
   A. I can see the sun.   B. I can see clouds.
   C. I can see birds.   D. I can see the moon.

For questions number 7 to 9, please look at picture C.

7. (**B**) Question number 7, where are the children?
   A. They are in the dining room.
   B. They are in the living room.
   C. They are in the movie theater.
   D. They are in the library.

8. (**D**) Question number 8, please look at picture C again. What are
they doing?
   A. They are watching TV.
   B. They are playing cards.
   C. They are doing homework.
   D. They are chatting.

9. (**A**) Question number 9, please look at picture C again. What is
between the plant and the chest?
   A. There is a television.
   B. There is a flower.
   C. There is a plant.
   D. There is a sofa.
   * chest (tʃɛst) *n.* 五斗櫃；櫃子

For questions number 10 to 11, please look at picture D.

10. (**A**) Question number 10, what are the older boy and girl wearing on their feet?

    A. They are wearing slippers.

    B. They are wearing sandals.

    C. They are wearing shoes.

    D. They are wearing skirts.

    * slippers ('slɪpɚz) *n.pl.* 拖鞋   sandals ('sændl̩z) *n.pl.* 涼鞋

11. (**D**) Question number 11, please look at picture D again. Where are the books?

    A. They are on the desk.

    B. They are in the desk.

    C. They are in the cupboard.

    D. They are on the bookshelf.

    * bookshelf ('bʊk,ʃɛlf) *n.* 書架

For questions number 12 to 13, please look at picture E.

12. (**D**) Question number 12, why is the girl falling down?

    A. She slipped on a bucket.

    B. She tripped on a shovel.

    C. She kicked a bucket.

    D. She tripped over a bucket.

    * bucket ('bʌkɪt) *n.* 水桶   shovel ('ʃʌvl̩) *n.* 鏟子
    trip over 絆倒

13. (**C**) Question number 13, please look at picture E again. What did she drop from her hand?

    A. She dropped her balance.

    B. She dropped a bucket.

    C. She dropped a shovel.

    D. She dropped a flower.

For questions number 14 to 15, please look at picture F.

14. (**C**) Question number 14, what is in front of the house?
　　A. There is a boy.
　　B. There is a postman.
　　C. There is a bicycle.
　　D. There is a car.

15. (**A**) Question number 15, please look at picture F again.　What is "A"?
　　A. It is a fence.
　　B. It is a house.
　　C. It is a mailbox.
　　D. It is a window.

　　* fence〔fɛns〕*n.* 籬笆　　mailbox〔'mel,bɑks〕*n.* 信箱

Part B

16. (**B**) Do you like the movie?
　　A. No, they are not interested.
　　B. No, it is boring.
　　C. Yes, it is interested.
　　D. Yes, it is boring.

17. (**A**) Roy is your friend, isn't he?
　　A. Yes, he is.　　　　B. Yes, it is.
　　C. He is.　　　　　　D. No, he is.

18. (**C**) Can you speak Chinese or English?
　　A. Yes, I can speak neither.
　　B. No, I can't speak neither of them.
　　C. I can speak both of them.
　　D. Either of them will do.

19. (**B**) How do you like it?
        A. Sure.
        B. I don't like it very much.
        C. No, I don't.
        D. Yes, I like it very much.

20. (**D**) How are you getting along?
        A. Oh, it's nothing.
        B. Any time.
        C. I don't mind at all.
        D. Not bad.

21. (**A**) May I come in?
        A. Please do.   B. Here you are.
        C. There it is.   D. Here it is.

22. (**B**) What time is it now?
        A. February 8, 1999.
        B. 9:22.
        C. Monday.
        D. Tomorrow morning.

23. (**B**) Why did you do so?
        A. By bus.   B. For fun.
        C. The smaller one.   D. A teacher.

24. (**D**) Mary, someone is knocking at the door. Who do you guess it is?
        A. It's not Jack, I am sure.
        B. It is my friend Tom that will come to see us.
        C. Jane likes to knock at someone's door.
        D. It must be Sue.

25. (**A**) Everything is on sale in the store today.
  A. How nice it is! Will you come with us?
  B. We will have that for nothing.
  C. You look great.
  D. We will pay for that.
  * *for nothing* 免費 (= *for free*)

26. (**C**) How much are the tickets, please?
  A. It is $3.00 every.
  B. They are sold out.
  C. They are $3.00 each. Children can get in at half price.
  D. The tickets are on the desk.

27. (**C**) When did you go there?
  A. Twice a week.   B. For two days.
  C. Last week.   D. In my office.

28. (**C**) Thank you for the present. It was just what I wanted.
  A. What did you want?
  B. I'm sorry you didn't like it.
  C. I am glad you like it.
  D. Was it a present?

29. (**D**) Is your sister sick today?
  A. That's all right.
  B. Yes, she's very well.
  C. It's all right.
  D. Yes, she's very ill.

30. (**B**) Where am I, please?
  A. By bus.   B. I am a stranger here.
  C. From China.   D. An American.

Part C

31. (**A**) M: I don't like this book very much.
    W: Neither do I.

    (TONE)
    Q: What does the woman mean?
    A. She agrees with the man.
    B. She doesn't know the book.
    C. She likes the book very much.
    D. She doesn't know what to do.

32. (**B**) W: I'm going to the bank, then to the dentist, and after that I have to prepare a presentation for my history seminar.
    M: I'd say you have a pretty busy afternoon.

    (TONE)
    Q: What is the man suggesting about the woman?
    A. She can go with him this afternoon.
    B. She has a lot to do today.
    C. She's almost as busy as he is.
    D. She might be finished by noon.

    * presentation (ˌprɛznˈteʃən) *n.* 介紹;發表
      seminar (ˈsɛməˌnɑr) *n.* 研討會;研習會

33. (**C**) M: Would it be better to buy a monthly meal ticket, or pay for each meal separately?
    W: What difference does it make? The price per meal is the same either way.

(TONE)

Q: What does the woman mean?

A. The man should buy a different meal ticket each month.

B. Individuals eat different amounts.

C. Buying the meal ticket won't save the man money.

D. The price of a meal varies from month to month.

* *meal ticket* 餐券

34. (**C**) M: I can't find the kind of jogging shoes I want anywhere in town.

W: Why not order them from a catalogue?　It's easier than running around town looking for them.

(TONE)

Q: What does the woman suggest that the man do?

A. Run in town.

B. Look more carefully.

C. Buy shoes from a catalogue.

D. Find an easier place to exercise.

* catalogue ('kætḷˌɔg) *n.* 目錄

35. (**B**) M: Do you think Professor Simpson will cancel class on account of the special conference?

W: Not likely.

(TONE)

Q: What does the woman mean?

A. She doesn't like the professor very much.

B. She doubts class will be canceled.

C. She doesn't want to attend the conference.

D. She wonders whether the professor is an accountant.

* *on account of* 因為;由於　　conference ('kɑnfərəns) *n.* 會議
  not likely 不太可能　　accountant (ə'kauntənt) *n.* 會計師

36. (**C**)　W: How is Marian's lab experiment coming along?
　　　　　　M: I'm not sure.　Why don't we go have a look?

　　　　　　(TONE)
　　　　　　Q: What does the man say about Marian?
　　　　　　A. He doesn't expect to meet her at the seashore.
　　　　　　B. He wants to know when she's coming.
　　　　　　C. He wants to see how her experiment is progressing.
　　　　　　D. He isn't interested in watching her.

　　　　　　* *come along* 進展　　progress (prə'grɛs) v. 進展

37. (**C**)　M: Gloria, are you going to send out invitations to the dance?
　　　　　　W: No, I got Dan to do it.

　　　　　　(TONE)
　　　　　　Q: What happened to the invitations?
　　　　　　A. Dan received them.
　　　　　　B. Gloria forgot about them.
　　　　　　C. Dan mailed them.
　　　　　　D. Gloria has sent for them.

　　　　　　* *send out* 寄出

38. (**B**)　M: Mitchell is the most talented actor on campus.
　　　　　　W: So he is.

　　　　　　(TONE)
　　　　　　Q: What does the woman think about Mitchell?
　　　　　　A. He's taller than anyone on campus.
　　　　　　B. He's the best actor in the school.
　　　　　　C. He's almost through with the campus tour.
　　　　　　D. He's studying at college to be an actor.

　　　　　　* talented ('tæləntɪd) adj. 有天分的
　　　　　　So he is. = *Yes, he is.* 他的確是。（加強語氣，附和對方）
　　　　　　be through with 完成；結束

39. (**A**) M: The math requirements for graduation are being changed.
　　　　　W: Yes, and I'm afraid I may be short one course.

　　　　(TONE)
　　　　Q: Why is the woman concerned?
　　　　A. She may need to take another course.
　　　　B. The math course is too short.
　　　　C. The graduation date has been changed.
　　　　D. She should have gotten a better score.

　　　　* requirement (rɪ'kwaɪrmənt) n. 必要條件；資格
　　　　　short (ʃɔrt) adj. 不足

40. (**D**) M: The doctor told me to quit drinking coffee.
　　　　　W: Shouldn't you quit drinking tea, too?

　　　　(TONE)
　　　　Q: What does the woman suggest?
　　　　A. Tea is better than coffee.
　　　　B. The man should switch to tea.
　　　　C. There are two reasons not to drink coffee.
　　　　D. The man shouldn't drink either.

41. (**C**) M: We have some openings in the sales department.　Are you
　　　　　　　interested?
　　　　　W: Do I have to have some sales experience?
　　　　　M: Not necessarily, as long as you like a challenge.

　　　　(TONE)
　　　　Q: What kind of job is offered?
　　　　A. Accounting.　　　　　B. Secretary.
　　　　C. Sales.　　　　　　　D. Guard.

　　　　* opening ('opənɪŋ) n. (職位) 空缺　　challenge ('tʃælɪndʒ) n. 挑戰

42. (**B**) M: You have to get off this road or turn around right away.

　　　 W: Am I doing something wrong, officer?

　　　 M: Didn't you see the "no-entry" sign?

　　　 (TONE)

　　　 Q: Who wants the woman to change her direction?

　　　 A. An officer worker.

　　　 B. A police officer.

　　　 C. A fellow passenger.

　　　 D. A bell-hop.

　　　 * *turn around* 轉向　　*no-entry* 禁止進入
　　　 sign (saɪn) *n.* 牌子　　bell-hop ('bɛl‚hɑp) *n.* (飯店) 服務生

43. (**C**) M: I'm going to join my family in Florida next fall.

　　　 W: That's nice.　I took my family there for sightseeing last summer.

　　　 M: Oh, really?　I can hardly wait for the family reunion.

　　　 (TONE)

　　　 Q: Why will the man go to Florida?

　　　 A. For research.

　　　 B. For pleasure.

　　　 C. To see his family.

　　　 D. For business.

　　　 * reunion (ri'junjən) *n.* 團聚

44. (**D**) M: I've just started subscribing to a magazine called "World Environment."

　　　 W: Really?　Does it come out every month?

　　　 M: Well, it used to, but now it comes out bi-monthly.

(TONE)

Q: How often is World Environment published nowadays?

A. Every week.　　　　B. Every month.

C. Twice a month.　　　D. Every other month.

* subscribe (səb'skraıb) v. 訂閱 ＜to＞　　**come out** 出版；發行
  bi-monthly (baı'mʌnθlı) adv. 二個月一次　n. 雙月刊
  publish ('pʌblıʃ) v. 出版

45. (**C**) W: You should know, Tom, that our new company policy
　　　　　　 says that you can smoke only in a designated area.

　　　　M: What if the smoking section is full?

　　　　W: Then use your own judgment.

(TONE)

Q: What does the boss mean?

A. Tom should quit smoking.

B. Tom should buy cigarettes.

C. Tom himself should think about where he smokes.

D. Tom should go outside.

* designated ('dɛzıg,netıd) adj. 指定的

Part D

46. (**B**) Bill likes traveling and has visited forty countries.　This winter
　　　　he went to Hawaii for his vacation.　He took lots of pictures,
　　　　but he left his camera on the airplane.　He hopes someone
　　　　will find it and send it back to him.

(TONE)

Q: What happened to his camera?

A. He forgot to take pictures.

B. He left it on the airplane.

C. He bought it in Hawaii.

D. Someone found it and sent it to him.

47. (**A**) Kate began to drive a car only last May and is still not very skillful. The other day she bumped into another car while trying to park at the supermarket. There was only slight damage to her car and none to the other one, so she immediately drove away.

(TONE)

Q: What happened to Kate's car?

A. She damaged it slightly.

B. She began driving it.

C. She parked it at the supermarket.

D. She damaged it seriously.

* **bump into** 撞到

48. (**C**) Mary and Jane planned to go hiking this weekend. On Saturday Mary got up very early, made a picnic lunch, and went to the station. She waited there for an hour, but Jane didn't show up. Finally, Mary realized they had planned to go hiking on Sunday.

(TONE)

Q: When did Mary go to the station?

A. An hour early.

B. To meet Jane.

C. On Saturday.

D. After her hiking trip with Jane.

49. (**C**) We apologize to passengers waiting for the 3:20 express for Norfolk. This train is running approximately 45 minutes late, due to a collision at a crossing on the southbound track between a local train and a truck.

(TONE)

Q: Where was this announcement made?

A. On a train.　　　　B. On a plane.

C. At a station.　　　　D. At Norfolk.

* express (ɪk'sprɛs) *n.* 快車
approximately (ə'prɑksəmɪtlɪ) *adv.* 大約 (= *about*)
due to 由於　collision (kə'lɪʒən) *n.* 碰撞
crossing ('krɔsɪŋ) *n.* 交叉路口
southbound ('sauθ,baund) *adj.* 南下的　　track (træk) *n.* 鐵軌

50. (**D**) And now business news. Consumer spending has surged 14.3% from last year's figures to $86.4 billion in the first quarter. Imports of consumer goods soared 36% to $22.7 billion in the same period.

(TONE)

Q: How much did people spend in the first quarter of this year in comparison with the first quarter of last year?

A. 1.1% less.

B. 36% more.

C. $86.4 billion more.

D. 14.3% more.

* surge (sɝdʒ) *v.* 快速上升　　soar (sor) *v.* 飛漲
in comparison with 與～相比

51. (**A**) The search continues for three-year-old toddler Betty Jarvis, who disappeared from a suburban Dallas park the day before yesterday. Her mother, Linda Jarvis, who was buying ice cream for her daughter when she disappeared, made an emotional televised appeal this morning to anyone who might have information on Betty's whereabouts.

(TONE)

Q: When did Betty Jarvis disappear?

A. Two days ago.   B. Yesterday.

C. This morning.   D. This afternoon.

* **toddler**（'tɑdlɚ）*n.*（走路走不穩的）小孩（= *child*）
   the day before yesterday 前天   **emotional**（ɪ'moʃənl）*adj.* 感人的
   televised（'tɛlə,vaɪzd）*adj.* 由電視播放的
   appeal（ə'pil）*n.* 請求   **whereabouts**（'hwɛrə,bauts）*n.pl.* 下落

52. (**C**) Thank you for calling Shears and Flowbuck. Store hours are Monday through Friday, 8:30 a.m. to 9:00 p.m.; Saturdays, 10:00 a.m. to 7:00 p.m.; and Sundays from noon to 5:00 p.m. Call 277-7996 for more information on this week's special deals.

(TONE)

Q: What number should you call to get more information?

A. 277-9967.   B. 276-2277.

C. 277-7996.   D. 279-7996.

* ***special deal*** 特價商品

53. (**C**) As I mentioned in my address last year, 1993 is going to be a year of change, not only within IBB, but also in the market as a whole. Moreover, it will be a crucial year for us—one which will determine our market share for the next ten years.

(TONE)

Q: Where is this address being given?

A. At a university.

B. At a high school.

C. At a large corporation.

D. In a government department.

* **address**（ə'drɛs）*n.* 演說   **crucial**（'kruʃəl）*adj.* 非常重要的
   market share 市場佔有率   **corporation**（,kɔrpə'reʃən）*n.* 公司
   department（dɪ'pɑrtmənt）*n.* 部門

54. (**A**)　The Brookfield Center officially opened today.　The seventy-five-story building is now the tallest in the city.　Begun in 1991, the center cost fifty million dollars, with about half of that amount coming from the state development board. Fifteen state officials, including the governor, attended today's opening ceremony.

(TONE)
Q: How many state officials were at the opening?
A. Fifteen.
B. Twenty-five.
C. Fifty.
D. Seventy-five.

　* officially (ə'fɪʃəlɪ) *adv.* 正式地
　　board (bord) *n.* 委員會　　***opening ceremony*** 開幕典禮

55. (**B**)　May I have your attention, please?　This is to remind everyone that we're getting new office furniture delivered today.　This means that all elevators will be used for the delivery, so please remember to use the north and south stairwells when entering or leaving the building.

(TONE)
Q: What are they having delivered today?
A. Computers.
B. Furniture.
C. Lunch.
D. Carpeting.

　* elevator ('ɛlə,vetɚ) *n.* 電梯
　　stairwell ('stɛr,wɛl) *n.* 樓梯井 (建物樓梯佔用部分)
　　carpeting ('kɑrpɪtɪŋ) *n.* 地毯料

56. (**C**) This is the *Weekend Review* with a look at what's new in the video stores. Herman Schwartz's most recent movie, *Violator IV*, has just come out on video. This one, if you pay attention to the plot, isn't much different from the first three Violator films. But who cares? Violator fans want action, action, action, and that's what they get—and plenty of it.

(TONE)
Q: What is this a review of?
A. A movie that will be on television this weekend.
B. A movie that starts showing soon at the theaters.
C. A movie that has just come out on video.
D. A movie that will be coming out on video soon.

* *video store* 錄影帶店   plot (plɑt) n. 劇情
   review (rɪ'vju) n. 評論   theater ('θiətə) n. 戲院

57. (**C**) The capital city of Indonesia is Jakarta. In the 1600s the Dutch came to Indonesia and built a trading post where the city now stands. Known by the name of Batavia, the trading post later became the headquarters for the Dutch East India Company.

(TONE)
Q: What is the old name for Jakarta?
A. Indonesia.
B. Jakarta City.
C. Batavia.
D. Dutch East India.

* *capital city* 首都   Jakarta (dʒə'kɑrtə) n. 雅加達 (印尼首都)
   trading post 貿易站   headquarters ('hɛd'kwɔrtəz) n.pl. 總部

58. (**A**) New Zealand has two main islands—North Island and South Island.　South Island, the larger of the two in area, is dominated by the mountain range that runs down it from north to south.　In mountain regions the weather changes fast, so warm clothing should always be carried, even in summer.

(TONE)

Q: What is true of the climate in the mountain regions?

A. It is usually cold in summer.

B. It is usually warm in summer.

C. It is both wet and cold in summer.

D. It is rarely cold in summer.

* dominate ('dɑmə,net) *v.* 支配；占大多數

　mountain range 山脈

59. (**A**) Smoking by teenagers is on the increase, British government figures indicate.　The British Medical Association has called for a total ban on cigarette advertising, a change in government policies on smoking in public places, and major increases in the price of tobacco.

(TONE)

Q: What would the British Medical Association like to have banned?

A. Cigarette advertising.

B. Government policies.

C. Price increases for tobacco.

D. Smoking-related diseases.

* figure ('fɪgɚ) *n.* 數字　　indicate ('ɪndə,ket) *v.* 顯示

　Medical Association 醫藥協會　　total ('totl) *adj.* 全面的

　ban (bæn) *n.* 禁止

60. (**C**) Exploding eggs may sound funny, but it's no joke.　When you cook eggs in the microwave, you should always crack them into a dish first, then poke the yolk before you turn on the oven.　If you don't, internal pressure can cause the egg or yolk literally to explode in the oven or when you start to eat.

(TONE)

Q: How can you prevent an egg from exploding?

A. Cut the egg with a knife after cooking it.

B. Turn the egg over while cooking it.

C. Break the egg and poke the yolk before cooking it.

D. Don't put the egg in a dish before cooking it.

* microwave (ˈmaɪkro͵wev) *n.* 微波　　crack (kræk) *v.* 敲破
poke (pok) *v.* 戳　　yolk (jok) *n.* 蛋黃
oven (ˈʌvən) *n.* 微波爐　　internal (ɪnˈtɜnl) *adj.* 內在的
literally (ˈlɪtərəlɪ) *adv.* 不誇張地；正確地

心得筆記欄

劉 毅 ^{高二}_{高三} 英文家教班 招生簡章

I. 上課日期： 秋季班（7月7日至12月19日）
　　　　　　春季班（1月5日至5月28日）

II. 開課班級：

A班：週三晚上 5：40～9：30　　　E班：週六晚上 5：40～ 9：30
B班：週四晚上 5：40～9：30　　　F班：週日上午 8：20～12：20
C班：週五晚上 5：40～9：30　　　G班：週日下午 1：20～ 5：20
D班：週六下午 1：20～5：20　　　H班：週日晚上 5：40～ 9：30

III. 學費： 7900 元（學費包括一切講義費、外國老師翻譯作文閱卷費）

IV. 獎學金制度：

- 各校班上學期總成績第一名，可申請獎學金 *3000* 元，二、三名獎學金 *2000* 元，四、五名獎學金 *1000* 元。
- 本班學期總成績前 400 名同學，都有獎學金或禮品鼓勵。第一名 *10000* 元，第二名 *9000* 元，第三名 *8000* 元，以下略。

V. 授課內容： 本班獨創模擬考制度。

根據聯考最新命題趨勢，蒐集命題委員參考資料，完全比照最新聯考試題編排、印製。

一般補習班，從名詞、動詞開始教文法，學到了介系詞，前面的名詞、動詞又忘了。前面背的單字，後面又忘，文法試題中的單字又太簡單，完全沒有整體的觀念，碰到聯考試題，沒能力答，也寫不完。即使是英文教授，沒有經過嚴格的模擬考的訓練，也沒辦法得高分。沒有訓練，就不可能在 80 分鐘內，又寫作文、又寫翻譯，還要做完 55 條選擇題。因此，

聯考得高分的唯一祕訣，就是：模擬考試➡上課檢討➡針對弱點加以加強。

有些同學剛開始考個二、三十分，經過考試磨練後，增加到五、六十分，聯考考到九十幾分。因本班每次模擬考試題，沒有重覆，考試只有 70 分鐘，一到聯考，考試題目重覆，時間又有 80 分鐘，所以自然能得高分。其他英文家教班想學，但學不會，因為他們沒有「學習出版公司」為後盾，資料不足，更捨不得花錢請外國老師改考卷。

作文翻譯不讓外國老師改，怎麼會進步？就像一個外國人寫的中文作文，可能請另一位外國老師改嗎？作文回家寫怎麼寫得下去？只有在課堂上那種考試氣氛，才能讓你專心答題，快速寫翻譯作文。知道自己的弱點，才能進步神速。

VI. 上課地點： 台北市重慶南路一段 10 號 7F　☎（02）2381-3148・2331-8822

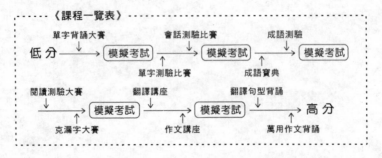

中級檢定英語聽力班 招生簡章

I. **開班目的**：協助考生中級檢定英語聽力測驗輕鬆過關。大學聯考未來加考英
聽，是聯招會既定政策，愈早準備愈好。

II. **開課班級**：

A 班	每週一 晚上 6：10 ～ 8：10
B 班	每週二 晚上 6：10 ～ 8：10
C 班	每週三 晚上 6：10 ～ 8：10

III. **收費標準**：*4800* 元（劉毅家教班學生優待為 *3800* 元）

IV. **上課方式**：完全比照研發中的「中級檢定英語聽力測驗」，收集出題內容，
每次上課考聽力 40 分鐘，培養同學臨場感，考後發詳解，並再
聽一次。並有老師隨堂說明講解。

◆●「中級檢定英語聽力班」報名表 ●◆

姓　名		電　話	
地　址			
就讀學校		班　級	

劉毅升大學英文家教班

台北市重慶南路一段10號7F（火車站前・寶島銀行樓上）
新電話: 2381-3148・2331-8822

Editorial Staff

● **主編** / 劉　毅

● **校訂** / 謝靜芳・蔡琇瑩・高瑋謙

● **校閱** / Laura E. Stewart

● **封面設計** / 張國光

● **打字** / 黃淑貞・蘇淑玲

|||||||||||||||●學習出版公司門市部●||||||||||||||

台北地區：台北市許昌街 10 號 2 樓 TEL：(02)2331-4060・2331-9209
台中地區：台中市綠川東街 32 號 8 樓 23 室
　　　　　TEL：(04)2223-2838

|||||||||||||||||||||||||||||||||||||||||||||||||

中級英語聽力檢定②

主　　　編／劉　毅
發 行 所／學習出版有限公司　　　☎ (02) 2704-5525
郵 撥 帳 號／0512727-2 學習出版社帳戶
登 記 證／局版台業 2179 號
印 刷 所／裕強彩色印刷有限公司
台 北 門 市／台北市許昌街 10 號 2 F　　☎ (02) 2331-4060・2331-9209
台 中 門 市／台中市綠川東街 32 號 8 F 23 室　　☎ (04) 2223-2838
台灣總經銷／紅螞蟻圖書有限公司　　☎ (02) 2795-3656
美國總經銷／Evergreen Book Store　☎ (818) 2813622
本公司網址　www.learnbook.com.tw
電 子 郵 件　learnbook@learnbook.com.tw

售價：新台幣一百八十元正
2003 年 3 月 1 日一版二刷

ISBN 957-519-532-9